MW01273285

Pour la belle
et douce Noëlla
que j'apprécie beaucoup!

Mélanie Lavy

Mélanie C. Larue

CHILD
OF THE SUN

ISBN (Print) 978-1-68222-594-3 (Ebook) 978-1-68222-595-0

CHAPTER ONE

My head was killing me. I didn't know where I was. I tried to look around me, but I couldn't see anything. They had put a bag on my head. I could see it was still daylight, but I had no clue of the time. I could feel the sun beating down on me. I was tied to some kind of a post. I tried to untie myself with my mind, but it didn't work. I could hear people talking from afar. I didn't recognise any of the voices. I felt powerless and alone. I thought of Antoinette, my deceased best friend, my only friend, and asked for her guidance and help, but in return there was only silence.

I heard footsteps coming closer.

"What's this, Seth?" asked an old man's voice.

"She's the one I was looking for, the one with the dangerous, glowing mind," replied Seth. I recognised his voice: it was the voice of the leader who had shot that poor, innocent little girl and kidnapped me from school. At the sound of his voice, I stood up straight, grinding my teeth.

"How do you know it's her?"

"Trust me. I know."

Someone approached me. He took the bag off of my head. In front of me, deep green eyes flooded my vision. I felt naked. I felt like he could read my mind, my whole life. Reading minds was an ability I had experienced all my life, but this was the first time someone else actually tried it on me, and I didn't like the feeling.

"She is still a child, Seth. She's not dangerous. Not yet anyway. How old are you, young lady?"

"Sssixteen," I replied with a weak voice. I was so thirsty, that my throat felt like sandpaper.

"What's your name?"

"Ashley Connors."

"Welcome to the Dragon Minds School. This will be your new home now. You will never go back home, for your own and your family's safety. I suggest you follow the rules and try to fit in... Otherwise, you will end up in the Dragon Minds Jail."

I looked into the big, brilliant green eyes of this odd-looking old man, who was probably in his sixties. He wore an apple green robe with a gold cape that stood out from the rest of the people who were all in black. I wondered if I could trust him. It stunned me that although he could read my mind, I couldn't read his. It's was the first time in my life that I couldn't read someone's mind.

"Excuse me? I am lost here. Where am I? And why am I here? I never requested to be at this school."

"You are on Dragons Island. It's not on the map. Nobody knows about this island, and we want to keep it that way. You are here because you belong here among us, in the wizard world."

"The wizard world? Excuse me, but I'm not a witch. I don't belong here. I'm just a genius. I belong in the Ancestral School."

"I beg to differ. You are not just a genius. You also have powers. You proved that today. A genius has brains, granted, but wizards have power. You have both gifts. That makes you dangerous," said Seth.

"How did she prove that, Seth? What did she do?"

"She can teleport objects for one thing, and she put some kind of protective shield around a little girl who I tried to shoot."

"Interesting," said the old man.

"Actually, he did shoot and kill one innocent little girl in cold blood prior to that, right in front of everybody at school," I said.

The old man stared at me for a while. He didn't look mad or surprise to hear that.

"Sometimes extreme measures are needed, young lady," the old man said. Then he turned his head and looked at Seth. "Seth, you can go back to your guardian's station. I'll take care of her from this point on."

He waited until Seth had left before he continued.

"My name is Master Thunderstone. This is my private island. I am the master of the wizard world. I have the most powerful powers among the wizards," he said. He was expecting a reaction out of me, but I had none, so he continued.

"My job is kind of like the president in the regular world. I make sure our people act, survive, and remain in a peaceful environment. We act in an underworld way, in the shadows of the cities, where nobody sees us." He lowered his voice so it was deep and scary when he mentioned the shadows of the city, as if he was trying to impress me or scare me or see my reaction. I didn't give him the satisfaction he was looking for; I simply looked him straight in the eyes.

"All mysteries in the world are the wizard's doing," he added. "We do it secretly for what we believe is right. We believe in justice and revenge. We don't believe in today's political system. The number one rule is to act and react without being revealed to anybody," he said, as though he had recited these statements over and over. However, that didn't convince me. But he was so absorbed in his speech that he didn't notice my disbelief. He just continued on and on. "That's why we had to find you and bring you here. You were starting to get too powerful, and word got out. We can't afford to be exposed to the real world...that would cause a war...and war is what we are trying to avoid. I know it's a lot to digest right now, but I'm sure you'll adapt in no time."

I didn't know what to say. I forced a smile. I had so many questions; I didn't know where to begin. I couldn't get over the fact that he ran a private island and a wizard school, yet a team of his people had coldly shot an innocent young girl in front of my eyes and kidnapped me earlier today. I was disgusted with these people, tired with this island already, and repulsed at their pretending that nothing bad had happen today, that they weren't cruel and dangerous people.

Master Thunderstone untied me, and I followed him. He started to show me the schools. There were different buildings in the backyard. Every building was a specific school.

"There are five different schools. You will have to go in each school every day. Here we call it schools, not classes, because every school teaches different powers and abilities. And in every school, we have kids from twelve to eighteen years old, in three different groups, divided by age. Your group will be from sixteen to eighteen years old. At eighteen years old, your scores will determine your field of work. You will automatically work for me. Got it?" he asked me, but I didn't respond. "In your free time, you will be free to go anywhere on this island, except the forbidden areas. You will soon learn where they are if you are an adventurist. Stay close to the school limits, and you will be safe. Miss Storm, the vice principal of the school, should arrive to give you a tour of the schools. I will see you at the sorting place right after supper," Master Thunderstone said before he disappeared.

CHAPTER TWO

I didn't even have time to ask him anything; in a blink of an eye, he was gone, leaving me all alone on the path. I looked around me. All I could see were butterflies flying from flower to flower. I didn't know where to go or what to do. I felt lost and alone on the island. I was about to turn around and retrace my tracks when someone teleported right in front of me.

"You must be Ashley. I'm Miss Storm, the vice principal of the schools."

As we walked on the beautiful one hundred-acre island, I notice that the trees were taller and bigger than the ones I was used to. The flowers too. There was what looked like a huge community garden. The first building was right beside it; it looked like a solid wooden cottage with wide, big windows. On the front door was a huge tree with thick roots carved on it. It was clearly the symbol of the school.

"This is the Grounding School where you will learn the benefits and functions of plants and the natural resources that surround us that can be used to create powerful serums for the island."

When we walked in, I was surprise to see how silent it was, but nobody was sitting at a desk. Students were scattered everywhere in little groups, reading from a big volume. I was impressed. They were all wearing green-and-yellow robes. All eyes looked at us, but everybody remained quiet. I was relieved that I could read their minds like regular people, even if they weren't pleasant to hear: "What is this freak show doing here? She doesn't look like a witch to me." "Now, Miss Goodie-Goodie just walked in…I mean, look at her! She looks like a nerd, not like a witch." "Go back where you belong!"

I didn't let it bother me. In fact, I was used to that treatment. You would think it's cool to read people's minds, but most of the time, it's not. People can be secretly mean, especially when you are labelled as "different" or "abnormal." It's human nature. I hear all their judgment, all their frustration, all their distraction…all their thoughts, good or bad. I don't like to be surrounded with a group people for that reason; it's too exhausting. And I don't have friends for that specific reason. The only true friend I had in my life was Antoinette. But she's gone now.

"Good afternoon, Miss Pomegrade. You will have a new student in your group C starting tomorrow. Everybody, meet the new recruit: Ashley Connors. I trust that you will help her feel at home."

"Wonderful!" said Miss Pomegrade with an intrigued look. She was studying me from head to toe with a smile on her face. Her voice was soft and soothing.

We continued on our visits to the schools. The second building was a big dome. On the front door was a big symbol of warriors with two swords placed in an "X" engraved in the wooden door.

"This is the Warrior School where you are going to train and defend yourself. Believe it or not, this school always comes in handy when you are working in the field, out on some kind of mission in the real world. This school's vision is bravery, quickness, and endurance, an asset for being a wizard. I believe this will be your particular group in every school. They are all in your age group."

When we walked into the dome, the atmosphere was very different from the Grounding School. The students were active, loud, and alert. They were dressed in black yoga-type suits. The boys' torsos were bare; the girls were wearing tank tops. A group of students was kickboxing, another was cardio training, a few were fighting with swords, and a fourth one was shooting targets with guns.

As soon as we walked in, the teacher called the students in. He whistled to get their attention, then screamed, "Listening position! We have company."

All at once, the students stopped what they were doing and gathered in a circle, standing still. The teacher looked very young. He was fit and well built. His blue-green eyes stood out with his tanned face and his black hair. His eyes fell on mine. They made me melt. He was extremely handsome.

"Mr. Corrigan. Meet our new student, Ashley Connors. She will be in this group starting tomorrow."

Unlike Miss Pomegrade, he didn't seem pleased to have a new student. He had such a serious look. It was impossible to know how he felt. I noticed that I couldn't read his mind; it was blocked, just like Seth and his partner's. I wondered what it meant. Only one thing came into mind: Even if I was attracted to him, I couldn't trust him.

"Students, meet your new teammate, Ashley Connors. I trust that you will make her feel welcome and that you will guide her for the first week," said Miss Storm.

And on that note, she turned around and continued her march. I could only follow her. I was relieved, believe it or not, to hear the minds of the students on my way out: "Not another girl!" "She looks so weak!" "She will never survive this school!" "You are my next victim." Even if hearing their thoughts was hurtful to me, I would rather hear their thoughts than be unable to. I had been afraid that I had lost my power of mind reading...I didn't like the feeling of being clueless.

On that last comment, I looked into the thinker's eyes. It was a red-haired boy, who was tall, big and had a partial smile on only one side of his face. I would have to watch my back with him around. His vibe was very neg-ative, almost too aggressive. I sensed trouble already.

Off to the third building, I could hear the waves from the shore. The waves were powerful. The peaceful sound made me feel nostalgic. I missed the Ancestral School. But the view of this particular school was spectacular. It was almost completely made out of glass. I was curious to see what this school entailed. I was surprised to see that although it was made of windows, I couldn't see what was inside. As we approached the school, there was a drawing of a circle of life with the words "Past, Present, Future, and Infinity" and a picture of flames and a rainbow in the middle of the circle. It was quite fascinating.

"This is the Healing School. Its vision is the cleansing of your body, spirit, and soul equals a perfect balance and a powerful mind. This will bring you deep in your past to heal the damage and release what is ready to be released. From the student's point of view, this is the hardest school. It is mentally challenging and drains your body's energy while you start releasing layers of your past until they are completely healed and cleared. It's a long process. But as you start taking weight off your shoul-ders, you will feel lighter and more powerful. The past can bring you to terrible and horrible places, but it's imperative that you learn to clear the past, the pain, and the tainted baggage of your past."

"Sounds painful."

"It is."

We walked in. There were many isolated chairs in individual narrow rooms, surrounded by window walls. All the students were tied to the chairs with metal chains. They all seemed to be in some kind of a trance. They each looked at the windows surrounding them. They all looked terrified. I couldn't see what they saw. Only they seemed to be able to see their past. However, I could hear their thoughts. They were all painful screams and negative thinking. I heard thoughts of murder, rape, torture, holocaust, and death. It made me want to run and scream.

At the center of the room was what seemed to be a control room with computers. A lady was watching the screens. I could hear her thoughts. She was able to see their past lives. That disgusted me. I felt like she was invading their past, their stories, their minds. I was not looking forward to this school. Not at all. In fact, I was terrified by it. All my life I had tried to hide my powers, live a secret life, and now my life would become an open book. That scared me; I didn't want any part of that. My life, my abilities, and my powers were my own business and nobody else's.

Miss Storm waved the teacher in. She abandoned her station and came walking toward us. She was dressed all in white. Her black hair and black eyes stood out on her face. She wore all kinds of jewelry with crystals all over her body. Miss Storm whispered, "Miss Grace, this is Ashley Connors. She will be a new student starting tomorrow. She will be in Group C."

"Welcome, Ashley. May your mind be a powerful one!" she said as she placed her hands in a praying position.

"We'll let you go back to your station. I'm just giving her a tour."

"It's a pleasure to meet you. See you tomorrow."

Then I heard her think, "Yeesh! Tons of layers to release. What an old soul...It should be interesting."

As soon as we got out of the school, I asked Miss Storm, "Do I have to go to all the schools? Or can I pick and choose the schools I would like to study in?"

"No, you have no choice in this. What scares you about that school?"

"I don't like the fact that she can see my past. I mean, my life is not an open book. I've always been introverted and reserved."

"Everything she sees remains confidential, don't worry. And she can only see what your soul is ready to release."

It didn't make me feel any better; I didn't like the idea of her—or anybody— invading my privacy. My past belonged to me; it was part of who I am. Spirits—because yes, I see spirits—kept reminding me to not forget who I was, where I came from, and now she expected me to erase my past? It wasn't going to happen. I'd have to figure out a way to deceive her. My head was pounding more than ever now.

Miss Storm walked at a very fast pace. She seemed to be in a hurry all of a sudden. I was pleased to hear her thoughts. "Hurry, you little nerd. I just want to go back into Mr. Charcoal's arms. It's the only time he's been in town, and you had to interrupt our fooling around in the storage room." I couldn't help but laugh out loud.

"What so funny?"

"Nothing. I laugh when I'm nervous."

"Well, try to restrain yourself. You are about to enter the fourth school, and Mr. Hunter doesn't know what laughing is. He is always grumpy and doesn't tolerate any signs of pleasure."

"What is this school about?"

"This is the Formula School. This is where you will learn how to make different kinds of serums. This school believes in brilliance, precision, and prevention."

"What kinds of serums?"

"All kinds: the traditional truth serum, the sleeping serum, the amnesia serum, the mind-blocking serum, the mission..."

"The what?"

"The mind-blocking serum. When you go out into the real world, you have to drink the mind-blocking serum prior to departure. It totally blocks your mind from your personal thoughts and your past. The only thing that stays in your mind is your mission. That way, if you ever get caught by an authority outside the limits of this island, they won't get any information out of you, even if they torture you or give you a truth serum. They will have no access to your mind."

I found that very interesting. It would explain why I couldn't read Seth and his crew's minds.

"How long does this serum last?"

"About forty-eight hours."

Standing before this high metal building, on the front door was the symbol of the school: a test tube with the words "pure," "precision," "prevention," and "protection" pouring down into a cauldron with some kind of recipe or formula in the background. When we walked in, the students were all wearing protective glasses and white togas with a gold collar. There was a white board at the front of the room, and on it was a title that read "Amnesia recipe." All of the students stopped what they were doing, and Miss Storm explained the unexpected visit.

"Mr. Hunter, this is Ashley Connors, a brand-new recruit. You can expect her in your class with Group C tomorrow." This last instructor acknowledged me with a nod but didn't say anything. At that, the vice principal turned around and left the school. I heard a student think, "Good luck! Mr. Hunter is a jerk!" Another said, "Great! Maybe he'll get off my case and be on this newbie's case instead." I could tell they were younger students. I wondered how they got recruited.

A question popped into my mind, but I waited until we were out before asking, "Are all the students recruited, or are some born here?"

"Most of the students were born here. A few were recruited under the age of twelve, and a very small number were recruited as old as you. One exception is Mr. Corrigan. He was recruited after he turned eighteen years old."

"Really? How was he recruited? Didn't he know he was a wizard?"

"Did you?"

"No."

"My point exactly. You know you don't fit in with the rest of the society, but you don't know that wizards truly exist. Or so he said. He is a brilliant mathematician and an even greater martial arts trainer. He can manipulate any minds and is the champion in any competition. But enough stalling, young lady. I have a busy schedule. Let's move on."

On the way to the fifth school, my mind was racing. Something didn't feel right here, but I couldn't put my finger on it. The fact that Mr. Corrigan could manipulate minds bothered me. How could I ever trust this teacher? Did he ever manipulate the students' minds? So what if he was good at martial arts? Was it a crime to win every competition? Or maybe he was alerting the human world of the wizard's world. I knew there was more to this story, but I didn't want to pry. One more thing was bothering me: Why did the name Corrigan ring a bell? Right! Collin Corrigan! Now I remembered! It was the other famous genius back home who was able to solve the aptitude tests just like me. Did he attend the Ancestral School too? I had to know. It was imperative to know.

I was standing in front of the fifth school. On the door was a picture of a tornado. In the tornado were mixed letters. I was immediately able to decode it. It said teleportation. "Cool!" I thought.

"This is the Teleportation School. Here we believe in the power of the mind to travel into the fifth dimension and the power of your energy to attract and repel objects like magnets."

"Really cool!" I said.

When we walked into the school, there were flying pencils and rulers everywhere. In the right corner were two students, trying to teleport from one corner to the other.

"Excuse me, Miss Travel, this is Ashley Connors, our new recruit. She will start school tomorrow in Group C." Miss Travel gave me a suspicious look, and I knew I would have to be careful with my powers around her. It felt imperative that nobody knew my unusual powers. My instincts told me my powers could get me in trouble.

It was easy to read Miss Travel's mind. She was here because she had nothing else to do. She didn't like children and hated teenagers even more. All she wanted to do was travel everywhere in the world. She was quite the adventurist, but she was stuck here under Master Thunderstone's orders, and she wanted to rebel.

"In what devotion is she?" Miss Travel asked Miss Storm.

"We don't know yet. The sorting will be done tonight, 7 p.m. sharp."

I read her mind. "Not again! I don't want to waste my time there! What do I care what devotion she belongs to? Oh, I'm so sick of this life! I can't wait to get out of here!"

Once we got out, I asked Miss Storm what the devotion was about.

"Everyone belongs to a devotion home. Each devotion home has its own philosophy and personality. Master Thunderstorm didn't explain this to you?"

"No."

"Well, it's a long story. Let's walk to the ring store while I try my best to explain it."

"A ring store?"

"Yes. It's required that every student have a ring."

"What for?"

"To have and keep more powers of course! You never used a ring?"

"No."

"Young lady, you have lot to learn here."

"Now about the devotion homes?"

"Yes. There are five devotion homes: the Brilliants, the Bravehearts, the Healers, the Powerful Minds, and the Nature Lovers. All attach to one school in particular. We normally call them by their related school names. There is always one that will stand out, that will attract you more, and that you will perform better in. It's written in your DNA. Tonight you will put your hand on the sorting scanner. The sorting scanner will read your lines and analyse your DNA. It will then automatically inflame the devotion home candle for you in front of everybody. This is our way to publicly announce your destiny. You have no choice in this. You will be entitled to a final sorting, by choice this time, when you turn eighteen. Your final scores will indicate the appropriate choice for you, but in the end, you will have a say in the one you choose."

CHAPTER THREE

When we walked into the ring store, an old man with a long, curly gray beard put his glasses on and greeted us.

"Hello, my dear. What allows me the honor of your visit today?"

"We have a new recruit. She's never used a ring before. We are here to find the perfect match for her."

"Well, of course! Come in! Come in!"

I started looking around, searching for a wand that would attract me. Personally, I thought rings were silly. I had never needed a ring for my powers. I wouldn't know what to do with it in the first place. I whispered to Miss Storm, "Do I really need to buy a ring? I don't have money on me."

"Money? We don't use money on this island. And yes, you have to have a ring, but you don't buy one. The ring chooses you."

"How?"

"Mr. Woodland, can you please explain to Ashley how this works please?"

"Certainly. Are you a righty or a lefty, dear?"

"Righty."

"Take your right hand and place it, palm facing down, above the rings. One in particular will fly into your hand just by reading your energy. This ring will be yours to keep. Take good care of it. It's a precious gift for wizards and witches. It could save your life."

I did what he asked me to do. Nothing happened. I walked everywhere in the store with my palm down, but no ring came flying into my hands. Mr. Woodland looked at me puzzled. I could read his mind: "That's impossible! She's not a witch. She doesn't belong here."

With a nervous voice, he said, "Try your left hand, dear."

I did the same procedure. Still nothing happened.

"Who are you, young lady?" Mr. Woodland demanded. "What do you want? You have no business here. Now get out!"

"What's going on, Mr. Woodland?" asked Miss Storm.

"This young lady is clearly not a witch. There is always one ring for every wizard and witch. It never fails. She must be a spy. We must have been breached."

"I'm calling Master Thunderstone right this minute," Miss Storm said.

She held me tightly by the wrist while she phoned Master Thunderstone.

"I'm under the impression that we have been breached. Come to the ring store."

Within ten seconds, Master Thunderstone and five guardians, including Seth, appeared in the ring store.

"What's going on, Doris? Andrew?"

"This young lady is not a witch. No ring suited her. No ring went flying into her hand," said Mr. Woodland.

"That's impossible!" said Master Thunderstone.

"That's what I said!" agreed Mr. Woodland.

"Seth? You brought her here. You said she had powers."

"Yes, she threw our guns in the air, and she threw a protective shield over a little girl. No bullets could go through."

They all looked at me in disbelief.

"How did you that? What are you?" asked Master Thunderstone.

"Look, I don't know if I'm a witch or not. I didn't know they truly existed before today. All I know is that I don't need a ring to have powers."

"What powers do you have?"

"Like Seth said, I can move things around. The protective shield thing, that was the first time I've ever done that. I don't even know how I did it."

Master Thunderstone looked deep into my eyes and pointed his ring with a big green stone in my right eye. Then he read his ring.

"My ring says you're telling the truth. But I want you to prove to me that you can move things around without touching them and without a ring."

So I did what he asked me to do. I moved the rings around. Rings were flying everywhere in the store. Mr. Woodland went ballistic and begged me to stop. I stopped only when Master Thunderstone asked me to stop. Rings were laying everywhere—on the floor, on the shelves, on the counter, even on people's heads.

"Look at the mess you've made! Look at my store! It was all neatly placed and now look! Look at my store! A pigsty! It will take a week to place everything back where it belongs!" screamed Mr. Woodland.

"This is outrageous! Ashley Connors, you will clean up your mess right this minute!" ordered Miss Storm.

"Sure," I replied.

I made all the rings instantly go back where they belonged. The guardians' mouths dropped. Mr. Woodland and Miss Storm stared at me.

"Impressive. Maybe she doesn't need a ring after all. Miss Storm, it's about dinnertime. Would you please escort her to the cafeteria? And could you kindly find her a table to eat at for tonight? I will see you all at the meeting hall at 7 p.m." said Master Thunderstone with a troubled and stunned tone before he teleported back to his office.

* * * * *

By the time we arrived in the cafeteria, the students and teachers were already sitting down. The teachers were whispering among themselves. But I could still hear them think. Apparently, news travels fast. They were discussing the events of the day: the ring store and me.

All the students were sitting at their proper devotion tables. Since I had no clue where I belonged yet, Miss Storm took her ring and used it as a microphone.

"Attention, all. I would like to present a new recruit. Her name is Ashley Connors. She doesn't have a devotion home yet as the sorting will occur at 7 p.m. I ask politely if anybody would kindly invite her over to your table just for tonight, even if she might not belong at your table."

Everybody looked at their empty plates. Nobody wanted me at their table. There were about 350 students, and not one student wanted me. Even though I used to be rejected all the time at school when I was younger, I had never felt more alone and out of place in my life.

"Well, we know that she will be part of Group C. I ask that one table in Group C would be kind enough to accept her at the table."

There were five tables for Group C. The same was for Group A and B. One for each devotion room, I figured.

Mr. Corrigan got up, used his ring, and said, "You should all be ashamed of yourselves. This is embarrassing. Bravehearts, make a place for Ashley at your table so we can all eat."

Like true soldiers, they obeyed their leader. I was kind of grateful, but not really. I was more embarrassed than anything. I sat down by the only three girls at the table and looked around. The red-headed guy was sitting right in front of me. He was studying me cautiously.

"Since the Bravehearts of Group C are the heroes of the day, they have the honor to go serve themselves with the teachers," said Miss Storm.

All the students at my table got up at once, plates in hand. I did the same and followed them. It was a big buffet with all kinds of international food. I hadn't eaten all day, but I wasn't hungry. I was too overwhelmed by the events of the day. This morning I was teaching in the Ancestral School (yes, I started to teach at fourteen years old because apparently I was smarter than the teachers). This evening I was an unwanted student in a wizard school. I just wanted to go to bed, sleep, and wake up the next morning, realizing that this was nothing more than a bad dream. I forced myself to put food on my plate. Every set of eyes was on me, observing my every move—even the teachers. Nobody talked while they were serving themselves. We all went back to our table in silence. The girl next to me made polite conversation.

"Hi, I'm Jenny, and this is Cecilia and Julie."

"Hi. Nice to meet you. I'm Ashley."

"Duh!" said the red-headed guy.

"Shut up, Steven!" said Jenny.

"You are lucky you're a girl because you would be dead by now."

I couldn't help but smile at her.

"So what devotion homeroom do you think you belong to?" asked Jenny.

"I don't know. This is all new to me. I didn't even know I was a witch up until today."

And on that, the table went quiet, like I had said something forbidden.

"What do you mean, you didn't know you were a witch? Are you stupid or something?" asked Steven.

"Yeah, really. I'm not saying you are stupid, but how can you not know by now?" asked the guy beside Steven.

"Honestly, I didn't believe in that crap. I thought it was all stories," I replied.

Again, I got the same look, the one that said they thought I was from another planet.

"Do you even have powers?" asked Steven.

"Sure."

"Then how can you not know you are a witch?"

"I just thought I was different, that's all!"

"Ha! Ha! Well, we know one thing for sure. You don't belong in the Brilliant devotion homeroom," said Steven. And at that, everybody laughed.

CHAPTER FOUR

The meeting place was a big auditorium. As it started to fill, I began to feel nervous. I couldn't believe all of those people were coming to see what devotion house I belonged to, especially because I knew that they weren't here by choice. Nobody really cared. It was just a silly tradition. I had no clue what devotion homeroom I belonged to. I wasn't convinced that I belonged among wizards either. On the stage in the center of the room was the hand-sorting scanner, the scanner that would choose my devotion house—my destiny, apparently. Behind the sorting scanner was a table with five big candles. Each candle had a different symbol to represent the five schools.

With the auditorium full, Master Thunderstone took the stand and said, "Thank you all for coming here tonight on such short notice. As most of you are aware, it's our tradition that every student and teacher be present for the event of sorting homeroom devotions. We are here today for the arrival of a new student, Ashley Connors. Tonight, the sorting scanner will publically announce Ashley Connors's best choice of devotion by DNA. Today, only one homeroom devotion will have a new family member. I trust that you will all greet her and welcome her like any brother and sister of the devotion house. Would someone be brave enough to demonstrate to Ashley how it's done?"

The auditorium went silent, but then Jenny walked up to the stand and put her right hand on the scanner. The scanner poked her index finger for a blood sample before it read her hand lines. After the scanner had finished reading her lines, the Bravehearts' candle magically flamed for everybody to see. The scanner screen cleared and became black within ten seconds.

Jenny invited me to the hand scanner, holding her bleeding index finger with her left hand. I could hear people making bets on what devotion I would be in; even teachers were discretely betting. My hands were shaking. I closed my eyes before I quickly put my palm on the scanner. A needle stung my index finger. It caught me by surprise; I wasn't expecting it to hurt so much. It was a big needle for a little finger! Strangely, the scanner was loudly reading my lines and made a weird nose, like an old loading computer, for a good two minutes before it finally inflamed all five candles. I could hear screams of surprise in the auditorium. Then everything went quiet. Everyone was in disbelief. I could hear their thoughts: "How can this be?" "What does it mean?" "What is she?" "First, no wand belongs to her, now this!" "Oh my God!" "How can she do that?" "I knew she was a freak!"

Here I was, in the middle of the stage by myself, my finger still bleeding. I put my left hand on the wound and asked my heart to make it stop bleeding and heal. Nobody could see what I did from the stand. My finger was like brand-new.

Master Thunderstone finally took his ring and placed it in front of his mouth. "Everybody stay calm," he ordered. "This is very unusual. Maybe the scanner needs to be rebooted or needs a new battery." He asked the janitors to kindly take care of that. All of this took about fifteen minutes, and I waited patiently while the crowd talked. I was still standing there alone when Mr. Corrigan and Miss Grace came to my rescue and took me off to the side, away from everybody's glare. Miss Grace took my right hand and was about to give me a Band-Aid when she realized my index finger was already healed. Her mouth dropped, and she showed my hand to Mr. Corrigan.

"How did you do that?" asked Miss Grace.

"I just asked my body to make the bleeding stop and heal my finger. Is that a crime?"

"Who are you really?" whispered Mr. Corrigan.

"Ashley Connors."

"Where are you from?" asked Miss Grace.

"I was born in California."

"What school did you go to?" whispered Mr. Corrigan

"The Ancestral School for Geniuses."

"Is that what you are, just a genius student?" asked Mr. Corrigan.

"Well, actually, I taught there since I was fourteen. I attended that school since I was nine. They didn't know what to do with me. I could pass every test with 100 percent."

"How did you do on your aptitude test?"

"I passed everyone one of them with 100 percent at fourteen years old. I was offered jobs, left, right, and center. That's when the principal offered me a teaching job until I was old enough to work in the real world, to do anything I wanted to. You are Collin Corrigan, aren't you?"

Mr. Corrigan looked me in my eyes. And then he tried something with me. He talked to me telepathically.

"Can you hear me?"

"Yes," I replied with my mind.

"You can never let people know about this gift. Do you hear me?"

"I figured that much. I've tried to hide it all my life," I spoke back into his mind.

"OK, we don't have time to explain, but do you think you can control flaming candles?" Miss Grace asked telepathically.

"I don't know, but I can try. Why?"

"It's best you don't know everything right now. You are not ready for this. But listen to me: If you can manage to control the candles, I want you to inflame only the Brilliants one," ordered Mr. Corrigan.

"Collin, this is too risky with Mr. Hunter. Like you said, she's not ready," said Miss Grace.

"Look, Grace, this is just what we need. Someone like her with Mr. Hunter. You know, keep the enemy closer."

"This is outrageous. She would be better off with you or me so we can keep an eye and watch her back."

Master Thunderstone came our way. Everybody stopped talking, even if we weren't actually talking.

"The sorting scanner is ready. Up again you go."

As I walked back to the stage, I overheard Master Thunderstone say, "What were you two doing with her?"

"We were keeping an eye on her, trying to get more information about her...just as a precaution, you know?"

"And did you find anything?"

"She went to the Ancestral School for geniuses, and she was rated number one."

"Thank you, Mr. Corrigan. It's good to know I can count on you two for the protection of the school."

"No sweat."

"Shall we?"

Once back on stage, Master Thunderstone took his wand and said, "May I have your attention please? Thank you for your patience. We are now ready for the sorting for the second time. Miss Ashley, you know the way."

I put my right hand above the scanner, and I closed my eyes. I said to my heart and my mind, for my own good, only let the Brilliants candle flare. I concentrated, and when I finally felt confident that I could do it, I put my hand on the scanner, letting the needle poke me for a second time. And to my great relief, only one candle lit: the Brilliants.

The Brilliants homeroom devotion stood up, screamed, and applauded. I looked for Mr. Corrigan, and he said to me telepathically, "Way to go, Ashley!" And then I heard Miss Grace say to Collin, "I hope you know what you are doing."

CHAPTER FIVE

After the meeting, Miss Storm escorted me to my new homeroom devotion house. The building itself was enormous and looked like a mansion.
It was divided into five sections, one for each devotion house. Every
section had separate locked doors, washrooms, a living room, and bedrooms. Nobody other than the devotion's students had access to it. In the
living room, students were studying everywhere in little groups. There was
a fireplace in the center of the living room, and everything felt cozy. Only
eight students of my age group were in this devotion. I was the ninth one.

The bedrooms accommodated four students each. Miss Storm assigned
me to an empty room. I would be alone for the time being, until a new
student joined us. The room was in a square shape. There were four single
beds with four dressers. Since I was alone, Miss Storm suggested that I
take the bed by the window.

I opened my dresser and found clothes inside it. Miss Storm had said they
were mine to keep. There were two pairs of pyjamas and two uniforms
for each school. There was also some kind of dress. I wondered what
occasion it was for. There were no jeans, no normal clothing, at least
nothing I was used to. I felt like I was in prison. No style, everyone was to
dress the same. It was depressing. I was never really into fashion, but this
was beyond plain and geeky. Was I supposed to wear these clothes on

the weekend? Was there a regular clothing store on this island? I would have to find out.

On my night table were my new schoolbooks and my schedule. I took a peek at it:

<u>Monday to Friday</u>
8:30–9:30: Healing School
10:00–11:30: Formula School
11:30–12:30: Lunch
12:30–1:30: Grounding School
1:45–2:45: Teleportation School
3:00–4:30: Warriors School

I placed everything in the backpack that was given to me. It felt weird to be a student again. I felt older than my age. It was true that I was only sixteen years old in my body, in this physical world, but my soul felt ancient. My head was still pounding, and all I wanted to do was sleep. I was supposed to go down to the living room after I was finished settling in my new room, but my legs couldn't move. My migraine was too severe. Both my body and mind were exhausted, and as soon as my head hit the pillow, I fell asleep.

* * * * *

I was floating again in the air. The stars guided me to the meeting place. I recognized this place. I'd been here before. It's was the Great Hall Community Center of Souls. It was all shiny with bright white marble columns. To my right, there was the Spiritual Learning Center. This was where I wanted to be. There were many cluster soul groups in the school. I knew which one was mine. My lifelong friends were all waiting for me, greeting me. It felt good to see them. I waved at them, smiling. They waved back at me. Just when I was about to get close enough to see their features, my guide pulled me out and brought me to the conference room. We were alone. Everything was quiet. I looked into her white light featureless face that kept changing forms. Sometimes it was a female human, and sometimes it was a white owl or a butterfly. Her voice was definitely female. Her name was Twilight. We were communicating telepathically.

"What brings you here, Ashley? You know it's dangerous to leave your body like this."

"It's not the first time I've left my body. I needed to escape. My world is crazy back there, and I am stuck in that body. I needed to breathe a little, have some fresh air."

"It's too risky. There's always a risk that you don't find your way back."

"I always find my way back."

"What if someone finds Ashley's body at the moment?"

"It's hard to be Ashley! Nobody likes me."

"You chose her body and this life, remember?"

"Yes, but I didn't think it would be that hard…"

"It never is…."

"I just needed to see some familiar faces, you know. I needed to feel loved and appreciated."

"You are not meant to join your soul group yet. Your mission on Earth is not done. You know your friends are with you in mind and in your heart. Remember who you are and why you were sent on Earth."

"It's clear now, but as soon as I will return in her body, my memory will be erased and I won't remember my mission."

"That's the nature of being human. You are stuck in a body with limitations. But your unconscious mind has an unlimited memory. Practice to *use your brain to its full capacity. You are doing well. You are getting stronger. Now go back into your human body before it's too late."*

"Can you let me remember this journey this time?"

"You know the rules. And you know your abilities are unlimited. Focus on one thing that will give you the energy and strength you will need. It's already within you."

"The sun."

"Good, focus on the sun."

CHAPTER SIX

I woke up at 6 am. It took me a while to remember where I was. I slept like a baby for once in my life. My migraine was also gone. I got up and went in the girls shower room. I was relieved to be the only one there. I didn't feel like chatting with anyone. In the shower, I relived the events of yesterday. There was so much to take in. How they came to take me from the Ancestral School, the death of the innocent girl, the five schools, the ring store, the devotion houses, Mr. Corrigan and Miss Grace...how strange they were acting and what they said to me. I had to find out more about my situation and why I had to choose the Brilliant devotion. Mr. Corrigan had said they could use someone like me in the Brilliant devotion. Why? What did he mean by "someone like me?" Who was I? And how come he could talk to me telepathically, but I couldn't read his mind? Could he read mine? How could I find out without revealing my gift to him? Could I trust him?

After my shower, I got dressed in the first suit: a plain, long white robe with a gold collar. I took my backpack and went to the cafeteria. I was the only student there, and only a few of the teachers were awake. Again, there was a buffet. I grabbed a plate and served myself. I was starving. I took a bowl of yogurt with cereal, a cranberry muffin, hash browns, and bacon. It was more than I would normally take, but I was starving. I didn't care.

While I was still filling my plate, Mr. Corrigan walked in. I desperately wanted to talk to him. I had so many questions. I purposely took my time, hoping he would come in to serve himself. He did, but he was very cold with me. He didn't even acknowledge me. I finally forced him to acknowledge me by saying, "Good morning!"

"Good morning!" he replied.

And that was it. I decided to try another approach. I tried to communicate with him telepathically.

"What would you like me to do in the Brilliant devotion?"

He pretended not to hear me, but I knew he did. I could see it in his eyes.

"What's so special about me?"

Again, no reply.

"Look, I know you can hear me, so..."

"Not now," he replied.

And then he left me there alone before I could say anything, with my full plate in hand. I went to sit on my own at an empty table. All the teachers were having breakfast now. Again, I felt all eyes on me, studying my every move. Mr. Corrigan purposely sat with his back to me so I wouldn't try to communicate with him.

I was done my breakfast at 7:20. I still had a good hour before my first school. The sun was shining outside. I decided to go for a walk and explore my new surroundings. The sun on my face felt good; it calmed my nerves. I breathed in its warm rays. I felt refreshed. I didn't know where to go, so I decided to listen for the sound of the waves. I wanted to go to the shore. I always loved to put my feet in the sea. The sound of the waves guided me. After fifteen minutes of walking, I could see the sea.

As I was getting closer, a beautiful colorful butterfly flew around my head. I put my hand out. It landed on my hand. Pretty soon I had a dozen butterflies on me. They were looking at me. I could hear them warn me, "Don't get any closer." I told them not to worry, that I knew how to swim. They said again, "The sea is a forbidden place. They are watching you." Just as they warned me, a big crow came by, and the butterflies flew away.

The crow landed just a foot away from me. Its eyes were freaky—they were bright red. His glare was unnatural. I also realized that I couldn't read its mind; in fact, it had no mind. I understood that it was a fake crow, spying on me. I pretended not to figure out what was really going on. I turned around and walked back toward the schools. The crow was slowly and discretely following me. I also noticed other crows flying around. I wondered what would have happen if I had reached the sea. I was curious to find out. I knew I had to watch my back. There were eyes everywhere watching me. If there were fake crows spying on this island, spying on me, what else would I find? What was hidden on this island?

By the time I got to the Healing School, it was 8:15. The door was unlocked, and I entered. Miss Grace, Miss Pomegrade, and Mr. Corrigan were whispering. I hid in the locker room.

"She's too young, Collin. She's not ready. She doesn't even know who she is yet," said Miss Grace.

"And don't forget, they are already suspicious about her. They are all keeping an eye on her," said Miss Pomegrade.

"Look, I don't care how old she is. She's our only hope. Maybe it's best that she doesn't know anything anyway. The less she knows, the safer our plan is."

"Don't be so cruel, Collin. She's on our side."

"Let's just keep an eye on her and try to help her as much as we can to prepare her for what's coming," said Collin.

"Shh! Kids are coming!" whispered Miss Pomegrade.

"Ok. Nine p.m., my school." said Mr. Corrigan.

I quickly hid behind the lockers as they went out of the school. As students were coming in, I got out of my hiding place and went inside the classroom. Everybody went to their usual chair. I was left standing alone in the middle.

"Good morning, class. You know the drill. Drink the pink liquid, sit comfortably in the chairs, and close your eyes."

All the students did as they were told. One by one, they were automatically handcuffed into the chairs. It looked like they were sleeping at first. But then they started to be tense, and most of them screamed. It looked painful. I was tempted to turn around and walk away when Miss Grace called my name.

"Ashley, follow me."

She brought me to an empty chair.

"This will be yours. I'll explain the procedure. First, sit down and drink the pink liquid."

"What is it?"

"It's a serum that will bring you back in your past. The more you do it, the deeper you will go into past lives."

"What are the ingredients?"

"It's a mystery, but don't worry, it's safe. It only activates your memory. It will help you dig into your subconscious mind."

"What's the purpose of this?"

"It's to clear any blockages and scars from your previous lives."

"And how am I supposed to do that?"

"It's up to you to find out. It has to come from you and only you. You won't be able to move on to a different past life until you manage to face your past and clear the damages. Do you understand what you have to do?"

"Yes, I think so."

"Good. Now drink the pink liquid and close your eyes. The rest will come naturally."

I drank the pink liquid. It tasted like strawberry. Instantly, I felt a wave of heat through my brain. I closed my eyes and sat comfortably on the chair. I heard a click and felt a cold metal around my wrists. I was hand-cuffed. I couldn't escape now. I had to face my past.

I was in the Ancestral School's cafeteria, hiding among all the students. Seth and his man had just shot the poor innocent student. I saw the little gifted girl killed in front of everyone because I refused to reveal myself. It was my fault. I saw the blood pool on the floor. I saw all the people that loved her and that she loved left behind in sorrow. I saw her spirit beside her body. She was looking at her body. She realized she was dead. She lifted her head and looked at me straight in the eyes. I felt terribly guilty about it. I acknowledged my pain and hers. It was clear to me what I had to do. I looked into the little girl's eyes through my tears, and I asked for her forgiveness. She smiled at me and said that I was forgiven. And then she added, "White Twilight is asking you to be brave, to trust yourself, and not to forget who you are."

The scene disappeared, and another one appeared.

This time I was nine years old. Kids at school were calling me names, pointing at me at recess. They even threw rocks at me. The teachers saw what was going on, but they pretended not to notice. They didn't want to interfere. They weren't fond of me; they felt threatened by my brilliance and the fact that I was probably smarter than them. The kids started to throw rocks harder this time. When I started to bleed and cry, a bigger crowd came around me to watch the show. I was the freak show. The teachers had no choice but to get involve now. They came running toward the crowd. But it was too late. I had to protect myself. I made the rocks fly in the other direction toward the throwers. They ran away. I got in trouble. I was brought to the office and was suspended for two days for throwing rocks at students. I still felt the anger of the injustice, the embarrassment of being the target, and the physical pain. I was cut everywhere. I had to let the painful memories go; they were dragging me down. I knew it was a good source of my incapacity for making friends. I opened my heart, and I knew what I had to do. I walked to the teachers and principal and said, "I forgive you for treating me unfairly." The teachers and principal looked shocked but accepted my forgiveness. I walked up to the bullies, and I said, "I apologize for throwing rocks at you, and I forgive you for bullying me at school."

The scene disappeared and another one appeared.

This time I was eight years old. My parents were gone for the evening. My brother was babysitting me. We decided to go to the park. He took his bike. Mine was broken, so I walked to the park. As I was walking alone, a bunch of older kids from my school came and grabbed me. They tied me to my house's front porch. They spray painted the walls with the words "Cursed child," "Witch," and "Freak show." They then opened my door and placed a bucket full of frogs in my house. They took a picture of *me at my house, and they left me there. I felt so small and humiliated, I wanted to die. I hated those kids, but I knew I had to replace this hatred with love to heal my internal deep wounds. I opened my heart. I saw bright lights come out of my heart. One by one, I met those students and told them that I acknowledged their frustration toward my odd abilities and I forgave them. I saw a bright light go up the sky before the scene disappeared before me.*

I was on the back of the quad holding Brandon, my best friend's cousin. He pointed to the deer in the bush. I felt at peace. The animals were so graceful and beautiful. Brandon held my hand. I remembered clearly this moment. I was fourteen. We stopped to wait for the other quads. I wanted to run away from this memory; I wanted to get out of this body; I wanted to forget this awful memory, but the memory kept cruelly flashing in front of me. Brandon took off his helmet, and I did the same. He was about to kiss me when we heard a horrible scream. We put our helmets back on and drove back to where we came from. We saw the scene of the accident. Antoinette lay dead in the ditch. I looked at her in disbelief. It took me a while to recognize her. Her face was covered in blood, and her left eye was missing. Her neck was in an unnatural position. I saw her spirit look at her dead body. She was not expecting to die. She lifted her head and saw me. She recognized me. I wanted to vomit. I felt so bad. I knew it was my fault.

I felt another heat wave in my brain. Time was out. The effect of the serum was over. Everybody was awake. My hands were free again. I was lost. I didn't remember what happened. Did I fall asleep? How long was I sitting there? What did I do? Did the liquid work on me?

"Good job, students. Time is up. Some student made some progress. Take deep breaths, and when you feel ready, you are free to go. I'll see you tomorrow," said Miss Grace.

I was the last one to get up. My hands were shaky, and my heart was racing. I wanted to know what had happened. Miss Grace came up to me.

"Excellent job, Ashley. You managed to clear three hurtful memories from this lifetime. This will balance your karma for your next life. How are you feeling?"

"Lightheaded. Confused. Shaky. I don't remember anything."

"That's how it's meant to be. Tomorrow you will face different blockages in your soul and memory. Congratulations! You accomplished a lot today."

I left the Healing School feeling light headed and exhausted. I felt like I had run a marathon. We had a half-hour break before the next school. It made sense. Most of students were lying on a hill, resting. The sun was shining, and it somehow calmed my nerves. I decided to go meet them. I lay by the group of students, trying to absorb as much sun as I could. It felt good on my body. It somehow rejuvenated me and gave me loads of energy. Jenny came over and lay beside me.

"Did you survive your first course of the Healing School?"

"Yes. It's exhausting, but now I feel better."

"I remember my first time; I had to rest for the rest of the day. Most people get sick the first week, just to warn you."

"Sick how?"

"Sick sick. The whole nine yards."

"Great!"

"This whole school is a waste of time. I've been going here for four years, and I only managed to clear six blockages. And I don't feel any better than I used to. Most students agree with me. The best students from the Healing School manage to clear maybe one life monthly. For the rest of us, it's a slow process."

"Hey, Jenny! Don't be a traitor! Stay on our side, will ya!" said Steven.

She looked at me apologetically and went back with her devotion school. I closed my eyes and tried to rest. I could hear two girls chatting beside me.

"I can't wait for the annual tournament this year. We are hosting the dance this year. Apparently, the Formula School hasn't hosted it for the last twenty years. This is huge. It's going to be amazing."

"Yeah, I know. For once, we can be represented by something else than just the brains."

"I wonder what kind of problems we'll have to face this year."

"I don't know, but it's always challenging. I hope we win first place this year. Wouldn't that be great with hosting the dance and all?"

"Oops! We better go! We can't be late with Mr. Hunter!"

Everybody got up at about the same time. I wondered what tournament they were talking about. I didn't care much about a dance, but a tournament, on the other hand, intrigued me. I figured I would have to try to be friends with them to find out about it.

When I got in the Formula School, everybody had their own place assigned, four students per table. Nobody tried to make a spot for me. Mr. Hunter looked at me and sounded annoyed that I wasn't sitting yet.

"Ashley, don't just stand there. Unfortunately, all the tables are full, but you can take this one," he said, pointing at the single table in the corner.

"Class, open your volume to page 248. Today's recipe is the amnesia serum. Follow the instructions. You will have to read between the lines for this one. It's full of traps, so beware! The first table to succeed gets one point. The last table to succeed loses one point. You know the drill."

A boy raised his hand.

"Yes, Frank?"

"What about Ashley?"

"No mercy with new students. You snooze, you lose. She starts at zero. You all have forty-five minutes to achieve the serum. Three, two, one. Go!"

Everybody raced to get the ingredients in the cupboards. I thought to myself, "What a terrible teacher—no modeling, no instructions, and no explanations." I opened my volume and read the ingredients. I took the time to read all the instructions. The inferring was simple to me. This should be a piece of cake. Once everybody was back at their tables, I went to the cupboard and took what I needed. I knew what to do and what not to do. It was obvious. Within five minutes, I was done with the serum. I raised my hand.

"Yes, Ashley?"

"I'm done."

"Impossible."

"How will I know if I succeed or not?"

"My ring will read it." replied Mr. Hunter, looking at me with suspicious eyes.

He pointed his ring at my serum. His stone turned green. His eyes opened wide in amazement.

"It's good. The point goes to Ashley." That was all he managed to say.

The students were murmuring something around me. I couldn't hear their voices, but I could read their minds. They were all shocked and jealous.

"How did she do it?" "What is she?" "We have to stop her!" "Who does she think she is? It's her first day, and she's already winning a point!" "Beginner's luck!"

Here I was again, the center of the attention. All I did was the recipe! Why were they all looking at me like I was a ghost or something?

"What can I do now?" I asked.

"You could try the recipes from pages 240 to 247."

I opened my book to page 240: the truth serum. This was so simple. In the next half hour, I had made seven recipes: the serum of truth, the serum of bleeding, the serum of coagulating, the serum of blindness, the serum of sneezing, the serum of fainting, and the serum of sleeping. Mr. Hunter was pacing the room. He couldn't stay still, he was so agitated. He didn't know what to do with me; he had never seen a student like me. He could not do it as fast as me, and that troubled him. He felt threatened by me. There were still fifteen minutes left. The students were all looking at me with curious eyes. They couldn't believe what they were seeing—and they couldn't believe how freaked out Mr. Hunter was. They thought it was hilarious seeing him like this. They didn't know what to make of me. I tried to avoid everybody's eyes.

I flipped pages and started to read the recipes. As I was flipping through the pages, old folded loose papers were hiding in the volume. I opened the paper and read the title: the lethal serum. It was written in codes, enigma, and riddles. It was clearly not for students' eyes, but it wasn't rocket science for me. Once you managed to decode the recipe, it was really simple. I just couldn't believe it even existed. If it fell into the hands of the wrong person, it could easily kill a large group of people.

The next one was just as shocking: the serum of destruction. The coding was more complex. When I was able to decode it, I was disgusted to see that it was an invisible aerosol, meant to kill anybody that would breathe the air. That serum could destroy a whole race, humankind and animals alike. This was a dangerous recipe. I couldn't believe it was actually placed in the school volume. Was it Mr. Hunter's volume? It just didn't make sense that it would be in the volume for every student to see. Did they have that serum in stock somewhere?

When Mr. Hunter realized what I was reading, he said, "Ashley, could you kindly step outside of the school? I need to talk to you alone."

I did as he told me. Once we were outside, he looked around to make sure nobody could hear him before saying, "What were you reading?"

"I was just flipping pages. Nothing in particular."

"Don't lie to me. I saw you. Give it to me. This is not for your eyes. Normally, nobody would be able to see anything. Only specific authorized wizard are capable of seeing this. How come you could see it with your bare eyes?"

"I couldn't. I saw nothing."

"You are lying! I saw your eyes scroll down the page."

"Look, Mr. Hunter, I don't know what you are talking about. I didn't see anything. It was just a blank page. I just noticed the page had a different color, that's all."

"What do you mean, a different color?"

"Well, all the pages are white, except that one in particular. It was ivory or a pale beige, that's all."

"You are such a liar! Nothing but trouble!"

"Excuse me?"

A crow landed on the front porch. Mr. Hunter whispered, "You may go back now, but I'll be watching you."

When I got back, time was up. None of the other students had been able to complete the serum in time. They all received a minus-one point. When the bell rang, I rushed out of the school. Before I got out, Mr. Hunter stopped me.

"Hand over the volume."

"But what about my homework?"

"No homework for you. You were able to complete the serum. No need to try to read between the lines to complete the task tomorrow. I will keep it safe for you and hand it back tomorrow in school."

I really didn't want to. I wanted to study the volume, to see if there were other hidden pages, but I couldn't think of an excuse to not give it to him. I took it out of my bag and handed it over. I had no other choice. "And don't even think about borrowing a book from a student. I'll be watching your every step. Good thing for me you are in my devotion homeroom."

And at that, I looked him in the eyes and tried to read his mind, but I still couldn't. He had it blocked. Another one. I would have to try to do the same or find a way to unblock it. Maybe there was a serum for this? I had to somehow get my hands on a volume, anybody's volume. I stepped out of the school and started toward the cafeteria. I needed to talk to Miss Grace or Mr. Corrigan, if I could find them.

The cafeteria was packed. Again it was a buffet. I searched for Miss Grace or Mr. Corrigan, but I couldn't see them at first. I walked toward the Group C section. Everybody's eyes were on me. I had left quite an impression in the Formula School. All of the devotion homerooms were curious about me. I tried to avoid their glare and searched for my table. Veronica, a girl from my devotion house, waved me to come sit by her.

"It's Ashley, right? I'm Veronica," she said, offering her hand.

"Nice to meet you, Veronica."

"So how did you do it?"

"Do what?"

"Make all those serums in the blink of an eye?"

"I don't know. I just read the instructions and followed them."

"You make it look so easy. What's your secret?"

"I have no secrets. I just listen to my heart, and it tells me the right answer."

"Yeah, ok. This is the biggest load of crap I heard today," said Stephany, the girl sitting beside her.

I saw Mr. Corrigan as he served himself lunch. I didn't let Veronica finish. I just stood up and started toward the buffet.

"Hey! Where are you going?"

"To grab some food! I'm hungry!"

"Well, wait for me!"

I didn't want her to follow me. I had to talk to Mr. Corrigan alone, but what could I say, really? I tried to listen to her, but my mind was somewhere else. Mr. Corrigan was in the donairs section. I hated donairs, but a girl had to do what a girl had to do. I went in the donairs section. To my disappointment, Veronica kept following me.

"A donair? Do you know how many calories are in these? You don't look like a girl who would eat big and fatty food like that, but hey, you go, girl!" said Veronica.

Distraction! She was distracting me. I needed to get rid of her if I wanted to talk to Mr. Corrigan. He gave me a quick glance. I held his glance and said, "Mr. Corrigan, I need to talk to you. In private."

"Oh, hey Mr. Corrigan!" said Veronica.

He just smiled at her—a fake smile.

"Mr. Corrigan, this is Ashley, the new student. She is an awesome serum maker. You should have seen her in school. She made...what? Seven serums in an hour?" she said, looking at me for my approval.

"You don't say?" he said, looking at me straight in the eyes.

"Mr. Corrigan, please, it's very important that I talk to you," I said telepathically.

"Not now" is all he managed to say before he went back to his table.

"Well, what kind do you want? You are holding up the line," Veronica said.

"You know what? I changed my mind. I don't want a donair after all."

"You're kidding!"

I walked to the soup and sandwich section. Veronica followed me there too.

"God, he is so hot!"

"Who, Mr. Corrigan?"

"Gosh no! Are you kidding me? Joshua!"

"Who's Joshua?"

"What? Just the hottest guy in Group C. Don't look his way."

"Well, how can I judge if I don't know who he is?"

"OK, to your left, the tall, broad-shouldered guy."

"Why don't you go talk to him?"

"I can't."

"Why not?"

"Duh! He's in the Warriors school."

"So?"

"We are not allowed to mix with different devotion houses."

"That's stupid! Why not?"

"The old saying, 'What happens in a family stays in a family.' And 'Family before pleasure.' Oh and the best one, 'You made your bed, deal with it.'"

"What about the old saying, 'Opposites attract'?"

"I like that idea, but it's crazy."

"No, it's not. Look, he is at the dessert section. Go there and choose a dessert. Make sure to make eye contact with him. I'll meet you back at the table."

Before she could say anything, I left her alone and went back to the table. She had left her books on the table. I looked around me. Nobody seemed to pay any attention to me. I took her pile of books and pretended they were mine. As soon as I put my hand on the formulas book, some kind of fly landed on my hand and bit me. I noticed it had tiny, laser red eyes. *Did I imagine the red eyes?* I wondered. I placed my hand back on the volume, and it bit me again...or I should say, it gave me a shock. I knew it had no brain, so I had no problem smashing it with my hands. When I crushed it, a little bit of smoke came out of it. I took the fly in my hand and examined it. Just like I thought, it was a little camera device. I put it on the floor and stepped on it. I heard a little crushing sound. *Now, that takes care of that!* I said to myself.

I took the book in my hands. I was about to open it when Mr. Hunter passed by and looked me straight in the eyes, warning me not to touch it. I put it back on the table. Veronica came back and sat next to me.

"I can't believe it! Our hands touched, and he looked at me!"

"That's great!"

"Yeah, I was reaching for a chocolate fudge square just as he was reaching for the same piece at the same time. His hand touched mine! He looked at me in the eyes and said, 'Excuse me, go ahead! Ladies first.' I think it's the first time he actually talked to me!"

She went on and on about Joshua. I pretended to listen, but I wasn't interested. My mind was somewhere else. I had to have a copy of the book and be by myself without any bugs or crows. Was anyplace a safe zone? I finished my sandwich and looked at the time. It was 11:52. I went to stand up, but Veronica stopped me.

"Where are you going?"

"To the washroom. Finish your lunch. I'll be right back."

I walked toward the teachers table while Mr. Hunter was serving himself at the buffet. I purposely slowed down in front of Mr. Corrigan, made eye contact with him, and said telepathically, "Going for a little jog. Meet me at the front of the building in two minutes." I didn't wait for an answer. I went outside. I pretended to tie my shoes while I was waiting for him. When I saw him around the corner, I started to jog. It didn't take long before he caught up to me.

"OK, make it quick and discrete," said Mr. Corrigan telepathically.

"I am being followed. I discovered something major in the formulas book, and now Mr. Hunter is after me."

"Do you think you can meet me at my school at 9 p.m. without being seen? It's not safe to talk here in the daylight. Do you think you can tele-port yourself to my school?"

"I'll try. Can you bring a copy of the formula volume?"

"Why don't you bring yours?"

"I can't. He confiscated mine."

"Fine, I will lend you mine. If you can't teleport, then don't try to walk to my school. You will get caught. And don't mention to anyone about our meeting…especially not Veronica."

And at that, he sprinted to his school. I was out of breath. I turned around and started back to the cafeteria to grab my backpack before going to the Grounding School.

* * * * *

When I walked into the Grounding School, the relaxing music soothed my mind. Everyone was sitting on the ground in a circle. Veronica was sitting with her group of friends, near Joshua's group. She had saved me a place beside her. I wasn't sure if I was annoyed or grateful for this. I was not used to all this thoughtful attention. It looked like she was trying hard to make friends with me, but I wasn't sure if I was ready for it yet, if I could trust her or handle another friendship ever again. Antoinette popped into my mind, and I instantly felt the pain in my heart. I tried to push her out of my head.

"Our task for the day is to search for a beauty white flower and find its functions, said Miss Pomegrade.

She showed us a picture of the beauty flower. "If and once you find one, you have to carefully dig it out with the roots still intact and bring it back to me. You have thirty minutes to complete the task. You are allowed to explore anywhere within the limits of the five schools."

Everybody went on immediately and randomly to explore the surroundings. Veronica asked me to join them, but I said I worked better alone, unconsciously keeping my space, guarding the walls that I had put around myself, to protect my heart. She looked disappointed and left with her friends. I took out my book and went to the index to find more about the beauty flower. It was on page 244. I opened the book to the right page and started to read about the flower. It mentioned its benefits and descriptions:

> Physical: essence of beautiful skin, nails, and hair.
> Emotional: helps build self-confidence and self-love.
> Spiritual: brings awareness and awakening.
> Magical: provides invisibility of unwanted area on your body
> (wrinkles, zits, scar, etc.).
> Habitat: shady and rocky ground.
> Height: 8 to 10 cm.

I closed the book, took a little shovel, and went to search for a rocky, shady area. I breathed in the sun's energy and looked in the sky. I let the sun guide me for shady places. It brought me near the forest. As I got closer to the forest, I saw a crow flying in circles above me. I concluded it was probably a forbidden forest. Right along the forest, there was rocky patch. I went to search for the beauty flowers. Sure enough, I found two beautiful white flowers.

"Hey, beauties! I need to bring you with me. I'll be careful," I said to the flowers.

I dug a circle around the flowers, making sure I wouldn't rip the roots. I carefully brought the flowers to Miss Pomegrade.

"Fantastic, Ashley! Now just fill in this descriptive flower sheet."

I was done in two minutes. I looked at my watch. I still had fifteen minutes left in the Grounding School. I asked Miss Pomegrade what I could do now.

"You can read the book. You can start with the benefits of the vegetation pages right before the index. I'm sure you will find some beneficial qualities worth searching for," she said with a wink.

I found the section in the back of the book. I didn't know what I was supposed to look for, but I skimmed down the pages. I stopped when I saw "blocked mind P. 320". I went to that page.

Rotten Ginger Root

Physical: relieves migraines.
Emotional: relieves anxiety.
Spiritual: helps communicating telepathically.
Magical: blocks your mind from mind-readers.
Habitat: isolated single plant in moist ground in the middle of old natural shrubs.
Depth: 2 feet in the ground.

Instructions: eat one rotten root like a carrot with a cup of water. For permanent effect, see page 45.

Beware: if taken by a natural mind-reader, it will double its capacity to read minds, and the person will be able to read even the blocked mind.

Interesting! I thought. I eagerly looked at page 45.

Root of Hibiscus

Physical: hardens the muscles.
Emotional: helps to stabilize your emotions.
Spiritual: third-eye amplificatory.
Magical: make any desired effect from any natural essence permanent. To be taken simultaneity with natural essence source.
Habitat: moist and fertile ground in full sun or partly shaded areas.
Depth: 6 inches in the ground.

I looked at my watch. I still had eight minutes.

"Find anything interesting?"

"Yes."

"Well, help yourself with what you need. Pretend to be still looking for the beauty flower."

"Thanks."

I looked around me. Right there, around the corner by the garden was a shrub of hibiscus. I took a shovel and ran. I started to dig around the shrub. The dirt was soft from the moisture. It was easy. I took a few pieces of roots and put them in my pocket while Miss Pomegrade was busy with another group of students. Then I quickly searched for a hidden ginger plant. Sure enough, right in the middle of the shrub, I found a little single plant of ginger. I started digging. It was hard with all the shrub roots in the way. I could hear my classmates coming back. Other teams had found beauty flowers. They were excited and proud. Perfect, my whereabouts and my mission were unnoticed. As soon as I extracted the root, I wiped it on my robe and bit it. It was soft and disgusting. I took a bite from the hibiscus root. This one was harder and tastier. I hid the rest in my pockets and walked toward the group.

"There you are!" said Veronica. "We found the beauty flower! How about you?"

I was about to say no when Miss Pomegrade said, "She sure did. She was the first one to find some."

Veronica looked impressed. I ignored her and asked Miss Pomegrade, "Excuse me. Could you tell me where the washroom is?"

"Yes, dear. Second door on the left."

I ran to the bathroom. I took another big bite of the ginger root and chugged it down with the fountain water. I then took a bite from the hibiscus root and so on.

When I came out of school, Veronica met me and said, "You are not feeling well, are you?"

"Not really."

"Told you. The first day finally caught up to you. Hang in there. Just two more schools for today."

Miss Pomegrade looked at me with suspicious eyes, almost like she was trying to read my mind.

"See you all tomorrow!" she said, still looking at me.

* * * * *

The teleportation was easier than I thought. We had to move things around with our rings. I could do it without one. I just had to look at the object intensely and ask my mind to move it. I got Miss Travel's attention.

"Ashley, come here. You are obviously wasting your time with this task. I want you to try to teleport yourself from one corner to the next."

Jealous eyes were following me.

"How? What do I have to do?"

"You rub your ring and connect with it. When you feel connected, you order your ring 'Travella' with the corner on your mind. If you concentrate enough, your body will teleport with your ring."

"I don't have a ring, Miss Travel."

"Right. You are the special student. Well, then I don't know if I can help you. Your magical ring, full of powers, connects with your own vibration and energy. Your ring and your hands become one, and the magical energy floats in your body until it meets your mind. It's a trilogy force."

"I'll try anyway."

"Suit yourself, but without the trilogy force, I don't see how it could work."

I did the same strategy that I used for moving things around: I had to focus on the corner and ask my mind to move my body to the corner. This was not new to me. I had been flying around the house since I was a kid, to my mom's despair. It worked! I teleported my body from one corner to the other. I was having fun. My mom used to hate it when I did that. I was teleporting to all corners of the room. I even dared to teleport myself onto my designated desk. The students were going wild. They burst out laughing when I landed on my desk.

"That's enough, Ashley. Try to teleport yourself outside the school and then come back." I did. "Try to teleport yourself to the cafeteria, take a coffee, and bring it back to me. And Miss Ashley, try not to spill it," Miss Travel said with a mocking tone.

When I came back with a coffee in hand within one minute, the students went quiet, and Miss Travel looked annoyed.

"You are wasting your time and mine. I will have to talk to Master Thunderstone. There is nothing I can teach you. Now sit back and occupy yourself. I don't want to hear or see you. I have a class to teach."

I opened the teleportation book. It was step-by-step instructions to how to teleport objects. The first step was how to connect with your wand and how to feel the waves of energy travel from your hand to your head. Then it was how to start moving a feather without touching it. How boring. I moved toward the end of the book. *How to teleport yourself from one building to the other.* I then went to the very last page:

How to teleport yourself outside of Dragon's Island:

This last step is the most dangerous one yet. You will need to know the secret access location to cross the seven protective shields. Your body will first need to be immune to the force field. These immune serums are in the hands of the secret agency and will only be given with the authorization of your master. If you attempt to teleport outside this island without the serum, you will die.

Miss Travel was right; there was nothing I could learn in this school, except to find out what the protective shields were and how to make the immune serums. But that wouldn't be in this school... that would be in the Formula School. If only I had the volume...I looked around me, and the students were all busy trying to make things fly. Veronica's bag was right beside me. I decided to try something. I asked my mind to bring

Veronica's formula volume to my hand. It worked, and to my great relief,
there was no fly this time. I opened the volume and looked in the index.
I was hoping to see the immune serums, but there was no such thing.
Nevertheless, something else caught my eye: the serum of duplicate
P.189. I opened up to the page:

The Serum of Duplicate

Function: transformation of a temporary duplication of any
living being.
Effect: from fifteen minutes to up an hour, depending on
the dose.

Interesting! I thought.

Ingredients: a teaspoon of fresh basil
1/4 cup of magic mushrooms
1/2 teaspoon of crushed pumpkin seeds
1/3 cup of blue algae
1/2 cup of roots of poison Ivy
1 cup of citric acid

Mix all of the dry ingredients together. Add the citric acid. Dip your wand
in the center and say, "Duplica." Shake well before drinking. While you
drink, look at the living being you would like to transform into. If the living
being in question is unavailable, a picture will do. For more advanced
minds, a clear image in your head might work.

Dosage: 1 tablespoon = 15 minutes
1/2 cup = 30 minutes
1 cup = one hour
Do not take more than 1 cup daily.

I took a mental picture of this page. It might come handy. In fact, I could
think of many reasons to use this serum. If only I could get my hands on
the ingredients...

I still had ten minutes left in the school. I made the book fly back into
Veronica's bag and took my grounding book. I searched for the

ingredients and where I might find them. I took note of it in my mind. By the time I was done, school was also finished.

"Ah, I really struggle with this school. I can't make things fly like everybody else. Thank God, the day is almost done. Off to the Warrior's School. Come on, hurry. Wait until you see Joshua in his suit!" Veronica said.

* * * * *

We went to change into the proper uniform. I couldn't wait to see if the roots had worked on me, to see if I could read Mr. Corrigan's mind.

As soon as I saw him, I got my answer. I heard his mind say when he looked at me, "Did she block her mind? She did! How did she manage to do that on the first day?"

God, he has such beautiful green eyes! I said to myself. He looked at me with his green eyes again. *Oops! Did he hear me? I will have to be careful with that...maybe he's a natural too....*

"OK, class, find your partner. You know the rotation. We are Thursday today," said Mr. Corrigan.

Veronica raised her hand.

"Yes, Veronica?"

"What about Ashley? Can she team up with me and Stephany?"

"Not today. Today she will work with me. I will show her the drill and how it works. Steven, can you supervise the martial arts today? Oh, and Mr. Justice is sick today. Christian, do you mind supervising the swords?"

They both agreed. Everybody was off to their respective stations. I was left alone with Mr. Corrigan. When he looked at me intensely, it gave me butterflies in my stomach.

"We will start with the training. Let's jog the track a few laps while I explain how it works."

We were jogging side by side when he finally talked again and pointed toward the martial arts section.

"This is the martial arts section. You will have to find a partner that matches you and practice your moves. The first few weeks, you will work with me while I show you the moves. To your left is the shooting range. It's pretty straight forward. You will have to aim and hit the center target. At first, it will be at close range. The better you get, the farther down the target goes."

After two laps, he brought me to the bicycle section. Side by side, we continued on. I couldn't help but notice all his muscles. They were distracting. I tried to ignore him. While we were biking, he said telepathically, "So you blocked your mind?"

"How do you know?"

"Because I can't read it anymore. How did you manage that?"

"Easy. I found the recipe in the grounding volume."

"Huh."

"Does it bother you that you can't read my mind?"

"Not particularly," he said, but his mind said otherwise. "Can you read mine?" he asked with hesitation.

"No. Yours is blocked too," I lied.

He was relieved to hear that. "OK. Off we go. Follow me."

We jogged toward the swords section.

"This is the swords section. I'm sure you are wondering why we have to learn that."

"Yes."

"Because if you ever have to battle another wizard, the sword is similar to a ring battle; it's the same technique. You have to disarm your opponent."

"I don't have a ring."

"Right, I forgot about that. You are out of luck for this one."

"Does that mean I don't have to do this section?"

"No exception. Not even for you, Ashley." teased Mr. Corrigan.

I was getting out of breath. He hadn't even started to break a sweat yet.

Then we heard a scream. We turned around and saw a student down, covered in blood. Jace was standing in front of him, white as a ghost, sword in hand. We both started running toward them. Christian was just standing there, pointlessly. Mr. Corrigan went down on his knees beside the injured student. It didn't look good. The sword had hit him in the stomach.

"Hang in there, Joshua. I'll call the ambulance. They will take care of you."

He took his cellphone and called the ambulance. I knew Joshua would die if we didn't attend to him right away. He was losing so much blood. Veronica crossed my mind, and I could imagine the pain she would be in if he died. While Mr. Corrigan was on the phone, I kneed beside Joshua and put my hand on his wound. My hand was covered in blood. I asked my heart to make the bleeding stop and to heal his wound. I felt electric energy in my hand. The bleeding stopped, and Joshua's wound started to heal. In ten seconds, it was healed completely. Joshua found his color again. Everybody looked stunned, including Joshua. He touched his stomach...Not even a scar!

I heard Mr. Corrigan say on the line, "Hummm. Never mind. False alarm. Yes I'm sure. It's just a scratch. Yes, I know, I'm sorry. Yes. Bye." He hung up and said, "Joshua, are you OK?"

"Yes, I think so."

"Can you stand up?"

"I'll try." Jace and Mr. Corrigan helped him up.

"Joshua, I'm so sorry. Mr. Corrigan, I didn't mean too. When I tried to disarm him, my sword touched him. I..." said Jace.

"You misjudged your distance. You were obviously standing too close to him. Christian, where were you? You were supposed to supervise to make sure this didn't happen," said Mr. Corrigan

"I was right there. I was tying my shoes when it happened."

"Hey! Didn't you just see what happen? Never mind the accident. I mean...what she did...that's impossible. I mean, I'm grateful she did it, but...how did you do it?" said Joshua, finally looking at me.

All eyes were on me now. Even Mr. Corrigan was looking at me with questioning eyes.

"It's sort of a...gift I had since I was a kid. It always worked on me. I never tried it on somebody else before. I'm just as stunned as you. I wish I would have known this before."

"OK, you guys. Let's call it quits for the day with the swords. Go join the cardio group for the remaining thirty minutes." They all looked relieved.

"Oh, and boys, look at my ring." And then he said, "Erasa memorisa." The boys stared blankly at Mr. Corrigan. "Boys, Mr. Justice is sick today. No swords for the day. Go join the group of training," ordered Mr. Corrigan.

"Yes sir!" they all replied.

It was my turn to look at him with questioning eyes.

"What? I just erased the last thirty minutes from their memory. They will be fine. It's best that way. Let's just keep your...gift secret for now."

He looked troubled. "Any questions about how it works in this school?"

"Yes. There are four sections. One for each day. What happens on the fifth day?"

"Friday is the day to compete with one another. We pick names, and you fight with the chosen adversary."

"Compete how?"

"We divide the class in two, and we rotate with kickboxing and sword fighting."

"Tomorrow is Friday. Will I have to fight?"

"Unfortunately, yes. There are no exceptions. If you want to be part of this group, you will have to fight. And trust me, you don't want to be an outsider here. You want to blend in, not attract attention. You've already attracted enough attention as it is. But I always leave my doors open until 8 p.m. If you want to train after school, you are free to come here. I can teach you then if you'd like."

"You will be too busy attending and supervising the fighting so a repeat of today's accident doesn't happen again."

"I'm usually by myself training. I'll be your personal trainer if you'd like."

"And what will it cost me?"

He looked at me straight in the eyes, debating if he should say anything or not, and then with a smile on his face, he said, "Your full cooperation and devotion."

CHAPTER SEVEN

"We are going up the hill to chill until the buffet opens. Care to join us?" said Veronica.

"Sure." I couldn't think of an excuse not to go. Besides, it was such a nice day outside, I could use a little bit of the sun.

The hill was crowded. Maybe it was the hangout for Group C. Who knows? I always hated crowds; they made me feel uncomfortable, and hearing everybody's thoughts was tiring. Like this morning, the hill seemed to be divided by devotion house. We, the Brilliants, were right in the middle.

"So how did you survive your first day of school?" asked Veronica.

"It was OK."

"That's an understatement!" said Julius, a guy from my devotion. "I'd say you had an awesome first day! You succeeded in everything. You made it look so easy."

"Yeah, really. I certainly would like to know how you do it," said Mel, another guy from my devotion house.

"I don't know. I just do it!"

"Just do it, huh?" Mel said, laughing at my comment. "Where are you from anyway?"

"I was born in California."

"California? Where is that?"

"You're kidding, right?"

"Ashley, Mel was born here, on this island," said Veronica.

"Born here, on this island?" I asked, stunned.

"Yup, born and raised here. More than half of the students are born here." And then he raised his voice and talked into his wand. "Attention, everyone. For Ashley's unawareness to this world, if you were born on this island, please raise your hand."

About three-quarters of the students from all five devotion houses raised their hands. I was shocked.

"We normally don't see wizards or witches at your age transfer into this school. Normally the transfer is done by the age of six years old, twelve at the latest. There are exceptions to the rules, of course. Look at Mr. Corrigan; he got transferred at eighteen two years ago. He never went to school here, but still he got his teaching job. A lot of wizards were mad about this. It caused a lot of commotion, but once we saw his skills and devotion, people calmed down. Now he is one of us," said Julius.

"How come he got transferred so late?" I asked.

"Good question. We were baffled by this. Apparently, he managed to keep his magical gifts to himself. He went to a school for gifted kids. Mr. Corrigan is a pretty quiet and reserved person, so nobody paid any attention to him—until he started to work, that is. Then people started noticing his unusual skills, word got out, and we found him by coincidence on a mission. There was Mr. Corrigan, fighting away like nobody else, winning every championship. I don't care how fit you are; you can't be that good without the help of magic," added Veronica.

"Why did you get transferred so late?" asked Stephany.

"I really don't know. They showed up yesterday morning and just...pulled me out of the school...killing a little girl in front of everybody," I said.

"What?" they all said.

"Yes. They killed her for no reason...just because I didn't reveal myself."

"You must be mistaken, Ashley. The wizards are not murderers. They don't kill for no reason. I'm sure she was guilty of something you are not aware of," said Veronica. The rest of them agreed with her.

"She was twelve years old! The problem was that I didn't even know they were looking for me, and they didn't know who I was. They took drastic, cruel measures just to capture me. I didn't know I was a witch before yesterday! If I would have known, she might not be dead today."

"This is bullshit! She's just pulling our leg," said Stephany.

"Ashley, you're kidding right?" asked Veronica.

"No!"

"I don't believe this for a minute. Wizards wouldn't just kill a kid. The real question is, how can you not know you are a witch?" asked Stephany.

"In the real world, we don't talk about wizards and witches, except maybe in children books."

"Then how did you explain all of your magical abilities?" asked Julius.

"I didn't try to explain them. I was a gifted child and an outsider all my life. I knew I was different, and I had to accept it. I had no choice."

"Gifted child, witch; same shit, different pile," said Mel.

"Actually, no, it's two different things. Gifted means unusual abilities, yes; but in terms of academic brilliance, gifted people have a higher IQ than the norm," I said.

"What? Speak wizard please," said Julius

"More intelligent in one specific domain or more."

"But with all that stuff you can pull, and without a *ring*, you can't tell me that's the norm."

"No, that's not normal. I was just kind of a genius."

Stephany rolled her eyes. I wasn't trying to show off or flatter myself, but that's how she felt. I annoyed her. She didn't like the fact that I was different and an outsider. The boys were curious about me—more because I was a new girl and they found me attractive. Mind you, Julius was attracted to anything that moved and was female. It was written all over his mind. Stephany was jealous because she was attracted to Mel, and Mel was paying more attention to me than her right now. Veronica didn't know what to think of me. She wanted desperately to be my friend, but she felt threatened by my differences. She didn't want to ruin her reputation just by hanging around me. She was very self-conscious, and she didn't know if I was good for her or not. Mel was simply curious and impressed by my abilities and hoped that I could teach him a few things. All the rest were trying to avoid me. They didn't know what to make of me. They thought the less they knew about me, the better it was for them. I didn't feel like I belonged in this wizarding world; I didn't feel like I fit in anywhere. All the students here were oblivious and immature to me.

"We know you're a genius. You proved that today. Is there anything you can't do?" asked Mel.

"There are many things I can't do."

"Such as?" questioned Mel.

"I can't draw for one thing. I can't dance. I can't sing. I am really not an artistic person."

I closed my eyes and tried to rest in the sun.

"So who are you going with to the dance?" ask Mel.

"What dance?" I asked, pretending not to know what he was talking about.

"The dance in two weeks, what else?" he said.

I looked at him blankly.

"You don't know about the dance, do you?" He sighed.

"Of course she doesn't know about it. She's not from here, Mel."

"Well, in two weeks, for the closing ceremony of the annual tournament, we are hosting the dance this year."

"What's the annual tournament?"

"Every year, Group C has two days of tournaments against the different devotion houses. The higher ranking devotion house team wins."

"What kind of tournament?"

"Different challenges. There is one tournament per devotion house. Some are always the same, some are different every year. We always start off with a tournament of the fabulios ball, representing the Teleportation House, and then—"

"The what?"

"Fabulios ball! You've never heard of that game? Girl, you have a lot to learn," said Mel.

"Well, tell me."

"We have two teams. The goal of the game is to score by placing the ball in the ring of the adversary team. You can't touch the ball with your hand or your feet, or any part of your body for that matter. You have to teleport the ball. But there are obstacles: walls move left and right, and floors elevate and drop at any given time, blocking access to the ring. The players must move only by teleportation and try to stop the ball by teleportation. After one hour, the highest scoring team wins."

"Sounds like fun."

"It's fantastic."

"No, it's not. It's nerve-wracking! And everybody is watching," said Veronica.

"OK, what else?" I asked.

"For the Formula Devotion, we always have to make a specific serum. It's never the same one. The first team to finish it successfully wins. For the Grounding School, they simulate someone with a certain disease, and we have to find a cure together, before the patient dies. We are not allowed to use our books in any part of the tournament. We can only rely on knowledge and common sense," said Julius.

"For the Warriors Devotion, we have to fight against each devotion house. The last one standing wins. For the Healing School, they simulate and play with one of our pasts, and we have to deal with it. The first team that is able to release that life wins. Miss Grace usually picks names for this one among the top students from each devotion house. Only one team-mate participates because we can't predict how long it would take to clear the past life.

"And finally, for the last tournament, the first team that steals the white flag wins. But to be able to get it, you have to face many challenges. You are allowed to use any kind of magic to succeed, and you can choose tools from any kind of devotion house. With this one, the team picks up to three players to face the challenges and steal the flag. This one alone lasts half a day," said Mel.

"And then it's the dance. We are hosting this year, so the décor and theme will be representing our devotion home," said Julius.

"You know, you still didn't tell me who you are going to the dance with," Julius said.

"Nobody. I told you, I can't dance."

"Ouch! Strike one, Julius!" said Mel.

At that, everybody laughed.

"Guys, time to go to the buffet, " said Veronica.

"Great! I'm starving!" I said.

CHAPTER EIGHT

When I walked into the school, Mr. Corrigan was training with a skipping rope. He was all hot and sweaty.

"Hey, you made it!"

"Well, it's kind of hard to leave with Veronica and her friends on my back. They didn't want to let me go."

"Yeah, I saw that in the cafeteria. Veronica can be quite monopolizing."

"Tell me about it."

He laughed.

"Well, I'm sure you didn't come here to chat, so let's get started. Put on those boxing gloves. They are a small size, so they should fit you. Come in the ring."

He jumped in like a deer jumps over a fence. I had to use both my arms to push myself in. "OK, the key is to always watch your opponent in the eyes. That way you will see his moves coming. Besides, you can read people's minds—that's always a bonus. Don't be the first one to hit. For a girl your size, it's best to wear out your opponent by dancing with him or her. Wait for his move, dance with him, and when he gets tired, then you hit him until he stops fighting. If you know he is going kick you from the left, either you jump or you hit him in the knee. Same thing goes for any kind of jabs or hits. Either you block him or you move fast and hit him on the other side before he touches you. You follow his every step, just like dancing."

"There's only one problem. I can't dance."

"Ha! Ha! Well, you're just going to have to learn. It's surprising what survival instinct can do. OK, put your hands like this, protecting your head and ready to charge."

I tried. He didn't like what he saw. He came behind me and placed my hands properly. I could hear and feel his breathing on my neck. He was so close to me, it gave me goosebumps. He went back in front of me, mirroring my position.

"OK, now look me in the eyes and hit me anywhere. Surprise me."

I looked him in the eyes. They made me melt.

"I can't. I don't want to hit you."

"Ashley, come on, hit me."

I didn't move. He kicked me in the left ribs. He was so fast and precise, but I saw it coming. His mind had told me. I ran to the right.

"Good. How did you know I was going to kick you?" he asked.

Right, he doesn't know I can read his mind now.

"I didn't know. It was simply reflexes."

I could tell he didn't believe me. He jabbed my right side. I didn't have time to move this time; he was so fast. I blocked it with my right hand. It hurt my arm, but I pretended not to feel anything. I had to stay alert—but his eyes were so distracting. He jumped into the air and did a three-sixty round-nose kick, aiming for my face. I quickly bent my body in half, avoiding his kick.

"See what I mean with dancing?"

He looked me straight in the eyes before he jabbed me in the face. I quickly bent back and sideways, avoiding his jab.

"Come on, Ashley, hit me!"

"I've never hit a person in my life. I don't have it in me."

"No?"

Within a second, he punched me in the ribs, leaving me out of breath. He took advantage of the situation and put one hand between my legs and the other one on my shoulders and managed to trip and push me down on the floor. He was lying on top of me and did some kind of wrestling maneuver, putting me in an awkward and painful position. I screamed in pain.

"Hit me, Ashley."

I did.

"Hit me harder."

I did. He let me go.

"What kind of punch is that? I didn't even feel it."

"I told you, I don't want to hit you."

"I have no problem hitting you...and you are a girl."

"Good for you!"

"Look, I could crush you and kill you in ten seconds if I wanted to."

"Good for you."

"My point is, you have to defend yourself. You can't just dance and take all the punches. You will lose or die," he shouted.

I looked at him with a defeated look. He held my glance for a couple of seconds. I heard him think, "God, her eyes! I could get lost in those eyes! She's even prettier when she looks mad. Why did she have to be so hot? It's just a distraction to my mission."

I didn't know what to make of this comment. What mission was he referring to?

Mr. Corrigan took my hand and said, "Come on." He took me to the back of the school where there were five punching bags. "Take this one and copy my moves."

I tried. He was punching so intensely and fast, I couldn't follow him. He slowed down. I punched, but not hard enough.

"You have the speed and the technique, but you need to hit harder, Ashley."

"I'm trying."

"Pretend the punching bag is your worst enemy."

"I don't have an enemy."

"Then pretend it's someone who's hurting a dear one...or worse, someone who is about to kill your loved one."

Antoinette crossed my mind. I pictured a man about to pull the trigger on her head. I punched so hard it hurt my hands.

"Again!"

I pictured Seth about to pull the trigger at the little girl. I punched even harder.

"Now we're talking! Whatever you were thinking about, use that in a fight…use that anger inside you. Now come back in the ring and hit me."

"Come on, I don't want to hit you."

"Pretend I'm the one who is about to kill a loved one. You can't hit me anyway; I'll avoid your hits. I just want you to try, that's all. Come on, dance with me, and then hit me."

"How romantic!"

He laughed. He started dancing in the ring, jumping around. I followed his every step. He tried to hit me in the ribs, but I avoided the hit. Then I quickly tried a jab in his ribs. He pushed my hands away.

"Good. Very good. And you're wrong—you are an awesome dancer."

"Not on a dance floor."

"I don't care about the dance floor. I care about the ring," he said, and he then looked at his watch. "Ashley, it's already eight o'clock. It's time to go."

"Should I just stay for our meeting?"

"No. Remember, they are watching you. They can't know about our meeting, and right now they know you are here. Pretend you are going to bed. Did you manage to teleport today?"

"Piece of cake."

"Great. Then I'll see you at 9 p.m."

"Don't forget my book."

CHAPTER NINE

I had taken a shower and put on an old pair of jeans and a black top. I placed some pillows under my blankets so it would look like I was sleeping in case someone would walk in. At 8:58 p.m., I closed my eyes and imagined the ring. I teleported right into the middle of the ring. I saw Mr. Corrigan, Miss Grace, and Miss Pomegrade already meeting around a round table, near the punching bags. Mr. Corrigan waved at me to come in.

Miss Pomegrade got up and gave me a high five. "Nicely done!"

"You're early," said Mr. Corrigan, looking at his watch with a serious look.

"Um...I could go back and wait in the ring if you prefer."

"No, no, you are here now. We were just talking about you," said Mr. Corrigan.

"About me?"

"Yes, you left quite an impression on the teachers on your first day. You were the talk of the evening," said Miss Grace.

"How so?"

"For starters, you managed to clear three layers today, which has never been done before. Then you managed to do seven serums in an hour, which has also never been done. Mr. Hunter was pretty upset about it. I've got to hand it to you, but he is also very suspicious about you," said Miss Grace.

"You've got to be careful, Ashley. You can't play the number one without being noticed. You have to play low profile if you want to survive out here," warned Mr. Corrigan.

"Let's not forget, you were also the first to find the beauty flowers, and I heard you also managed to teleport inside and outside of the Teleportation School on your first attempt," said Miss Pomegrade.

"Oh and by the way, Miss Travel asked Master Thunderstone if you could be excused from her class. That has never happened before. So yes, you left quite the impression," said Miss Grace.

"And the most impressive thing I have ever seen is when you managed to stopped the heavy and deadly bleeding and heal a wound right in front of my eyes with your bare hands," said Mr. Corrigan.

"What?" said Miss Grace and Miss Pomegrade.

"Yes, I had to erase memories today to cover up a miracle!"

"Oh, my God!" said Miss Pomegrade.

"Now we are debating if we should trust you at all. This is all pretty unbelievable. We don't know what to make of you. You are very powerful, and we want to make sure we can trust you before we say anything to you. We can't afford to compromise our mission," said Miss Grace.

"Hey, I didn't ask to be here, remember? They stole me from my school, my job, my life without my consent," I said, raising my voice.

"Your job?" asked Miss Pomegrade.

"Yes. I was a teacher at the Ancestral School for Gifted Kids since I was fourteen years old."

"She's right. She didn't want to be here. She didn't even know this island existed," said Mr. Corrigan

"How can you be so sure?" asked Miss Grace.

"Because I read her mind yesterday. She was pretty confused and freaked out about this place."

"How do we know she will be on our side, that she won't go tell everybody what we are up to?" said Miss Grace.

"Come on, Grace, that's not fair. Give her credit. She hasn't done anything for us not to trust her. She is the hope we were waiting for. Yes, she is powerful and unpredictable, but that's exactly what we need, what we are missing for the mission. We need her, and you know it. The clock is ticking; we don't have much time left. I want her in! Now who's with me?" said Mr. Corrigan.

Miss Pomegrade raised her hand. Miss Grace rolled her eyes but raised her hand too. She said to me, "Don't make me regret this."

"OK. What do you need me for exactly?"

"Before we start on this, tell us what you found out today at the Formula School?" said Mr. Corrigan.

"I think Mr. Hunter accidentally gave me his volume. Inside were some top-secret folded papers. Inside was hiding a formula for a serum of destruction and one for a lethal serum."

"Are you sure about this?" asked Mr. Corrigan with an intense and serious look.

"Yes. The coding is very complex. It says that it's an invisible aerosol, meant to kill anybody who would breathe the air. That serum could destroy a whole race, humankind or animals. This is a dangerous recipe."

"I can't believe it is actually in the school volume. It just doesn't make sense that it would be in the volume for every student to see" Miss Pomegrade said.

"Well, actually, apparently no student could have read it."

"What are you talking about?" asked Miss Grace.

"I guess it looks like a blank page. The letters are apparently invisible, but somehow I could see and read it. Like I said, I think Mr. Hunter accidently gave me his volume; he wouldn't want to lose his secret recipes. When Mr. Hunter realized what I was reading, he went ballistic. He took me outside the school and asked what I was reading. I told him nothing because it was a blank page. He didn't believe me at first. He said he saw me skimming the page. I said that I had simply noticed that it was a different color. Then the spying crow flew around, and he stopped talking and went back inside. That's why he confiscated my volume."

"What spying crow? What are you talking about?" asked Miss Pomegrade.

"There are crows flying around, spying on us. They are artificial and serve as cameras. Didn't you know that?" I asked.

"No."

"I did," said Mr. Corrigan.

"There are flies too. They bit me twice, trying to take Veronica's formulas book in the cafeteria."

"That's insane!" said Miss Pomegrade.

"Where have you been all these years? They have been around for a long time," said Mr. Corrigan.

"My question is, do the authorities have that serum in stock somewhere?" I asked.

"Very good question," said Miss Grace.

"Indeed. We knew they were up to something bad. We just didn't have any proof yet," said Mr. Corrigan.

"There's also the lethal serum," I added.

"Well, that's what we figured, but we don't have any proof," said Mr. Corrigan.

"It says it on another blank page."

"Are you sure about this?" asked Miss Grace.

"Yes. I think that they not only know how to make them, but they also have some in stock. Why else would Mr. Hunter be so anxious and worried about me finding what I was reading? Why else would he have confiscated the blank pages and my volume if he had nothing to hide?" I said.

"Good point," said Miss Pomegrade.

"If that's the case, and if your theory is right, we have to find out where the serums are and destroy it before they destroy the world. And this is why we need your help, Ashley," said Mr. Corrigan.

"What do you need me to do?"

"We knew from the start the key was to have a spy in the Formula School. We just never found a qualified and trustworthy enough person for this until you came on the island. This is why I wanted you to choose this school. Miss Grace already has connections with the secret agency. I have connections with the defense agency, and Miss Pomegrade controls the growth and protection of the natural resources on this island. If something suspicious is up, one of us is bound to find out. We've covered all the basis—or we've tried to. Thanks to you, we can now confirm that the lethal serum is not a myth and that there is also the serum of destruction. Can you remember the ingredients?"

"Yes. It's quite simple once you manage to decode it. For the lethal serum:

1. Fresh black mold
2. Poison ivy
3. Bee venom
4. Tarantula venom
5. Scorpion venom

"And for the serum of destruction

1. Lethal serum
2. Fire
3. Rat poison
4. Natural gas
5. Fuel

"Wow! That's terrible!" said Miss Pomegrade.

"How can we possibly destroy this?" asked Miss Grace.

"We need to find their hidden place as soon as possible." said Mr. Corrigan

"I agree, but until we do, we should make sure they can't produce more of this serum," I said.

"And how are we supposed to do that?" asked Miss Grace.

"Are there tarantulas and scorpions on this island?" I asked.

"Not in the wild, if that's what you are wondering," said Miss Pomegrade.

"Then how can they find the venoms?"

"Well, we do have an insectarium on the island," said Miss Pomegrade.

"What?" asked both Miss Grace and Mr. Corrigan.

"Yes. Insects are part of nature, and they are very useful for the cycle of life," answered Miss Pomegrade.

"Yes, but tarantulas and scorpions. Really? Are they really useful on this island?" Mr. Corrigan asked.

"Apparently they are very important for the wrong reasons on this island. Do you have access to this insectarium?" I asked.

"Yes. I have the keys."

"Then you need to get rid of them," ordered Mr. Corrigan.

"I can't just get rid of them. That would look too suspicious."

"She's right. We could fool them by extracting the venom and replacing it with water or another safe liquid. They won't know the difference," I proposed.

"Now you are talking," said Miss Grace.

"There's only one problem. The authorities already extract the venom. They keep it in a safe place; I'm assuming in the laboratory in the secret agency's building," said Miss Pomegrade.

"Then we need to somehow break in," suggested Mr. Corrigan.

"Good luck with that one," said Miss Pomegrade.

"You are forgetting that I have connections with the agency," said Miss Grace.

Mr. Corrigan rolled his eyes. "Yes, you have connections to get in the building, straight to Mr. Pump's office and into his arms."

Miss Grace blushed.

"Even if you get in, Mr. Pump won't let you wander around by yourself," Miss Pomegrade pointed out.

"I have an idea. This may sound crazy, but we could use the serum of duplication, and I could become a butterfly or something and..." I proposed.

"What's the serum of duplication? What are you talking about, becoming a butterfly?" asked Mr. Corrigan.

"The serum of duplication is a serum that enables you to duplicate a living being for up to an hour. That should be enough time for me to explore the building. I need to transform into a small living being, small enough to be in Miss Grace's pocket. A butterfly would be perfect because nobody wants to crush a butterfly," I said.

"How do you know so much about the serum? You've been here for just a day," said Miss Pomegrade.

"I read it in the volume."

"And how are we supposed to get our hands on this serum?" asked Miss Grace.

"We can make the serum. I know all the ingredients and the recipe, and Miss Pomegrade can give me the ingredients," I said.

"A-plus for effort, Ashley, but this is crazy. Ten thousand things could go wrong with you becoming a butterfly! If time runs out and they found you there, that would be the end of you," said Mr. Corrigan.

"We won't accomplish anything if we don't take risks, Mr. Corrigan. Besides, it's my ass on the line, not yours," I explained.

"Fair enough. Grace, what can you tell us about the building so Ashley could buy time?"

"Not much. Like you kindly said, I go straight to his office, and that's the third floor, second door on the left," said Miss Grace.

"My guess is, it would be somewhere where there's no window, probably in the basement," said Miss Pomegrade.

"I beg to differ. That would be the first place someone would expect to hide it. So they would do exactly the opposite. I'm thinking in a safe in Mr. Blake's office," said Mr. Corrigan.

"Who is Mr. Blake?" I asked.

"The president of the secret agency," answered Miss Grace.

"If it's in a safe, then it's pointless. Even a butterfly can't go in a safe," said Miss Grace.

"I have a better idea. What if I duplicate myself into a tarantula, and you say it had a baby? Make up a story about their reproduction or something. I'm sure they don't know anything about tarantulas. You could extract my venom—I promise I won't bite you—then call them and arrange for them to come pick it up. By the time they would come, I could transform myself into a butterfly, and I could hide in the case. They would bring me right to where we need to go. I would be able to spy to know for sure where it is. You, Miss Grace, would have to meet your connection at precisely five thirty. That way, on your way in, you could open the front door and let me out before I transform into myself. Then we can go from there."

"This is outrageous! Too risky!" said Miss Pomegrade.

"We have nothing to lose!" I said.

"We don't, but you do," replied Mr. Corrigan.

"Well, I'm willing to take the risk."

Everybody went silent.

"Miss Pomegrade, here are the ingredients. By the time I get to your class tomorrow, make sure you have all the ingredients ready for me. Have a pot ready for me. It's a simple recipe. I'll go to the bathroom and make the recipe. Then at lunchtime, I will come and duplicate into a tarantula. You will have to take a picture of me as the tarantula, then extract my venom. You will have only 15 minutes to do so before I become Ashley again...so that nobody will be suspicious about my disappearance. Then later, you phone them and arrange a pick up time right after school, say at 4:45."

"I don't know Ashley...this is all so soon...I need to think about this." said Miss Pomegrade.

"What is there to think about? If we want to eliminate those serums, we need to act now." I replied.

CHAPTER TEN

I see saw a teenager boy, Tom, crying over a dead body on the side of the road. I knew the dead body was Tom's best friend, Bryan. I knew Bryan was me. Tom was drunk, driving. He was speeding, racing another car, and crashed into a post. The impact killed me. I knew I was dead. I could feel Tom's deep remorse. I knew what I had to do: I needed to forgive him and tell him that I loved him.

Another scene appeared in front of me. *This time I was a military helicopter pilot. I had a crew of twelve men with me. The helicopter got hit. I lost control and crashed in the enemy territory. The helicopter exploded. We all died, each man leaving a family behind. I failed them all. I asked their spirits and their love ones to please forgive me. They accepted my apologies.*

I was a little five-year-old girl. I was hiding in my closet. My dad was very mad at me. I didn't do the dishes when he asked me to. He was drunk. He wanted to hurt me. He was looking for me. When he came in my room, I couldn't help but cry. He heard me. He opened the closet, took me by my ponytail, and started punching me like a raged man until I was knocked out. I hated my father. But I knew this feeling was not sane. I needed to replace it with love and forgive my father. When I told him that I loved him and that I forgave him, he fell on his knees and cried.

I was an abusive father and husband. My wife was badly bruised. My son hated me. He had a broken arm, thanks to me. I lost control last night. I recalled the events of last night. The baby wouldn't stop crying, and I lost it. I threw him against the wall and knocked him out. He was still in the hospital. Anger and impatience were eating me alive, like poison in my veins. I breathed in fresh air and breathed out a cloud of negativity. I replaced the empty space with brighter light with higher vibration—the vibration of love, patience, and compassion. I kissed my wife and my kids and told them that I was sorry, that I loved them with all my heart, and that I was going to take some anger management courses.

I was a slave. I was a housekeeper for a white rich family. I work sixteen hours a day in their mansion. If I was sick and slacked off a little bit, my master hit me with a belt. The lady of the house was never satisfied. She was always mean to me. The man of the house, a hypocrite senator, made me carry heavy loads of wood to keep the house warm. He made me sleep in the corner of the kitchen so I could get up in the middle of the night and keep the fire burning in the stove. He never allowed me a day off. He didn't pay me because I was black. I was not to talk unless spoken to. I was not allowed to eat with them or to sit with them. I had to use the outhouse; I was not allowed to use their fancy toilet. I had an inferiority complex. I was unworthy in the eyes of white people. I was a victim of injustice and racism. I felt my embarrassment, and I replaced my frustration, humiliation, and jealousy with confidence, happiness, and gratefulness. I opened my heart, and I forgave them.

Brandon took off his helmet, and I did same. He was about to kiss me when we heard a horrible scream. We put our helmets back on and drove back to where we came from. We saw the scene of the accident. Antoinette lay dead in the ditch. I looked at her in disbelief. It took me a while before I recognized her. Her face was covered in blood, and her left eye was missing. Her neck was in an unnatural position. I saw her spirit look at her dead body. She was not expecting to die. She lifted her head and saw me. She recognized me. I wanted to vomit. I felt so bad. I knew it was my fault. I knew this would happen, and I didn't do anything to prevent it. I was crying so hard. I couldn't see through my tears. I loved her so much. I was so ashamed and mad at myself. I told her that I loved her, that she was the best friend I could ever have, and that I was so sorry for not knowing it was her who was going to die, that I didn't recognize her. I told her I wished it were me who was dead, not her.

The effect of the pink liquid wore off, and I woke up. Time was up; Healing School was finished. I don't remember what I dealt with, but from what I could tell from Miss Grace's mind, I had cleared five past lives and was blocked again on one specific painful memory from this life. I still couldn't remember anything. She posted the top five students who made progress this week on the board:

> Ashley Connors: cleared nine layers and five past lives.
> Jonathan Vimy: cleared two past lives.
> Jon Hash: cleared one life.
> Stephanie: cleared two layers.
> Andrew: cleared one layer.

Everybody was looking at me with jealousy and suspicion. Miss Grace was actually annoyed by my performance. When our eyes met, she asked me telepathically, "Are we still on for today? Do you still feel brave enough to do this?"

"Yes, I am as ready as I'll ever be."

"Try to keep me posted."

"Will do."

Our secret conversation was interrupted by Veronica. She grabbed me by the arm and pulled me out of the school and guided me toward the hill again.

I lay down and closed my eyes, absorbing today's shy sun.

"How are you feeling today?" asked Veronica.

"OL, I guess. Just a little tired."

"Of course. So how did you manage to clear nine layers and five lives in two days?"

"I don't know. it's not like I remember any of it."

"Are you sure about that?"

"Yes. What is that supposed to mean?"

"It's just that everything seems too easy for you. You must have a trick that you don't want to share."

"No, I don't." On that note, I stood up and walked away.

"Ashley! Wait!"

But I kept going. I had too much on my mind to deal with jealousy. I was the first one at the Formula School. The door was still locked. It didn't take long before Veronica, Julius, Mel, and Stephany came to meet me.

"Ashley, I didn't mean to offend you. I am sorry if I did. We just never met someone like you before. It's just a little unsettling, that's all," said Veronica.

Mr. Hunter opened the door and let us in. He had put my table right beside his desk. He obviously wanted to keep an eye on me. On the board was the laughing serum. Everybody rose at once to grab the ingredients. I asked Mr. Hunter for my book. With an amused smile, he gave me a photocopy of the page. I was done with the recipe in five minutes. He dipped his ring in the serum; it turned green. He looked at me with an amused smile.

"Another point for Ashley. Ashley, would you give us the honor to test your serum?"

"No, thanks."

"Are you afraid that you didn't do it right?"

"No. I know it's good."

"Then why won't you prove it in front of the class?"

"With all due respect, sir, school just started, and the students need to work. This would only be a distraction."

"I sense some reticence in you. Are you all brains and a party pooper?"

Everybody laughed at his comment. I didn't reply.

"I'll test it, Mr. Hunter," said Julius.

"And here is the party guy with no brains—your opposite, Ashley. Sit down, Julius. Try to create the serum this time, and maybe I will let you."

"What can I do now?" I asked Mr. Hunter.

"You are excused from class."

I left the school and went straight to the Grounding School. When Miss Pomegrade saw me, she excused herself from the class and came to talk to me privately.

"What are you doing here? You are early."

"Mr. Hunter excused me from school. Do you have everything ready?"

"Yes, it's in the bag in locker twelve."

"OK, thanks. I'll go do it in the bathroom. Make sure nobody comes in."

I went to the bathroom and took my time making the serum. I had to wait until 11:30 before taking the serum. I couldn't do it now when Miss Pomegrade was teaching another group anyway.

When the bell rang, I hid in the bathroom. When every student was gone, Miss Pomegrade came to meet me.

"Are sure you want to do this?"

"Yes, let's get this done and over with."

"Come in the back of the class. We need to teleport into the insectarium. Hold my hand."

"OK. On three. One, two, three."

"Please don't hurt me."

"I won't. Here goes nothing."

I drank the serum, visualizing a tarantula. It tasted awful. I felt a sharp pain all over my body, from the inside out. Then I felt like I exploded, but I had just transformed into a tarantula. It felt really funny being that small. The room seemed very different and big from this angle. Miss Pomegrade looked like a giant from here; in fact, everything was huge and tall. I could hear every little sound and see all the dust on the floor.

Miss Pomegrade was looking at me with worried eyes. She was freaked out. Her voice was shaking when she said, "OK, Ashley, try to stay still. I'll try to be gentle. I hope it doesn't hurt too much. I..."

"Just do it. We don't have much time," I replied telepathically.

She seemed relieved that I talked to her. She pulled out a needle and took me with gloves on. She inserted the needle in my lower back. I felt a sharp pain. I felt like screaming, but no sound came out of my mouth. It lasted a good ten seconds, then she took the needle out.

"There, it's done. How are you feeling?"

"Like a tarantula in pain."

"Sorry. Now we just have to wait ten minutes for you to transform back into Ashley."

"Did you take a picture of me beside the other one?"

"No, I forgot. Let me go get the camera in my purse."

I walked awkwardly toward the other tarantula. It felt funny to walk with eight legs. The other tarantula looked at me like I was a freak, jumping at the sight of me, than cautiously walking toward me.

"OK, hurry, Miss Pomegrade. It's freaking me out. It's staring at me with hungry eyes."

"Oh dear! Smile for the camera!" she said, laughing out loud at her joke.

"Well, hello, pretty girl. Come here often?" the tarantula said to me.

"Not staying long. Back off."

"Well then, let's not waste any time. Come closer, pretty girl. I won't bite."

I tried to run away from it, but it kept chasing me around.

"Oh, dear! Oh, dear! Hang on, Ashley. Shouldn't be too long now…"

When it finally caught me and put its four front legs on my back, my body ached again. I was slowly transforming. When I transformed into myself, the tarantula was still on my back. I panicked and said, "Take it off! Take it off me!"

With her gloves on, Miss Pomegrade gently took it off and put it back in the exhibit.

"I hate spiders!" I said, still feeling it on my back.

"Good job, Ashley. Now off you go, before your absence is noticed. I suggest you teleport in front of the cafeteria."

"OK, thanks. I'll meet you back at 4:45 sharp. Remember to arrange the pick-up."

I teleported in front of the cafeteria. Luckily, nobody was there. My legs felt funny. My face was sweaty. I was dying of thirst. When I walked in the cafeteria, Mr. Corrigan looked at me, trying to read my mind. He wanted to know if everything had gone well so far. I discretely give him a thumbs-up. He nodded, then looked away. He was trying so hard to look disinterested, but he couldn't fool me. He was dying to know the details. Mr. Hunter was staring at me. I tried to ignore him. I went to my table, pretending nothing had happened.

"There you are! I looked all over for you," said Veronica.

"I went for a walk and fell asleep in the sun."

"You look sweaty. Are you feeling OK?"

"I'm fine, just thirsty."

I got up with my plate and my glass and went to get a drink of ice cold water. I chugged it and filled the glass again. I went to grab a bowl of soup. Mr. Corrigan joined me and grabbed a bowl of soup as well.

"So, did it work?" he asked telepathically.

I could see that Mr. Hunter was still staring at me, trying to read my mind. Master Thunderstone walked in and had his eyes on me too. He sat right next to Mr. Hunter. I decided it was best not to answer Mr. Corrigan. I tried to avoid his eyes.

"Talk to me, Ashley. Is everything OK? You look sick! What happened?" again telepathically.

"Shh. Not now. They are watching me."

"Care to go on a jog after your soup?"

"Give me ten minutes."

I went to sit at my table. I purposely sat with my back to the teachers to avoid their glare.

"Gee, Ashley, you look terrible!" said Mel.

"Gee, thanks."

"No, I mean, you are still pretty, you just look...exhausted."

"Pretty, eh?" teased Stephany.

"Shut up!"

"I am. I feel like I've been run down by a train."

"I told you the first week is tough," said Veronica.

I was still very thirsty. I chugged my glass of water again.

Mel grabbed my glass.

"You want another one?" he asked.

"Sure. Thanks!"

I could see Stephany was jealous. She already hated my guts. If only she knew Mel was not my type; she really had nothing to worry about. I'm not sure what my type was, but someone definitely more manly and mature. Mr. Corrigan popped into my mind, but I tried to push the thought away. I finished my bowl of soup and ate a piece of bread. When Mel came back, I saw Mr. Corrigan leaving the cafeteria. I quickly drank my water and stood up.

"Where are you going now?" asked Veronica.

"Going for a jog...hoping it will wake me up."

"That's a bad idea. You should be resting. Besides, you just ate," she said.

"Exercise is the best way to gain energy, for me anyway."

And with that, I walked away before she could say anything else. Mr. Corrigan was stretching outside, stalling. He waited for me to tie my running shoes before he started to jog. I had to run to catch up to him.

"Relax. Everything went well. I transformed into a tarantula. Miss Pomegrade did what she needed to do. The other tarantula wanted to reproduce with me, but I retransformed myself just in time."

He started laughing. "You are crazy, you know that?"

"I've been called worse things before."

"You sure you are up for this afternoon? You look terrible...I mean...not terrible—you still look the same—but you look tired."

"I feel terrible, but that's not going to stop me. We need to stick to the plan if we want anything done. Shit, look to your left, two o'clock."

He did. A crow was coming our way.

"Meet me at my school after supper," he said before sprinting away. We couldn't afford being seen jogging together; that would look suspicious. He was long gone by the time the crow came flying around me. I turned opposite from the way Mr. Corrigan had gone. Like I suspected, the crow was following me. I was getting out of breath, but running felt good. I decided to have a little bit of fun with the crow. I started zigzagging between trees so it wouldn't have a good view of me. The crow was trying to follow me as best as it could, but it eventually hit a tree and fell to the ground. I said to myself, "One down!" Satisfied, I went back to the main trail and walked back to the cafeteria.

* * * * *

At the Grounding School, as soon as we walked in, Miss Pomegrade told me telepathically that it was a go. I was grateful that today's mission was to find plants that would give us energy and take away growing pains. I thanked her. It didn't take me long to realize that I needed to find some adaptogen herbs like rhodiola, coffee, and shizandra to provide critical support to the body, to promote energy, and to reduce sensitivity to physical stress and pain. I ate all three herbs and brought back some to the teacher. I felt better within five minutes. She suggested that I keep some samples in my pockets in case I needed them later.

Again, I was the first one done. She let me study for the remaining time. I took out my formula volume, hidden in the back of my bag. I opened the book randomly to the serum of ascension. There was a big warning on the page:

To be taken with caution! High risk of death! Only people with higher brain activity will succeed. These herbs will help your spirit ascend out of your body, leaving your body behind and intact. This will permit your spirit to travel to other planes or to a specific place without being seen by others. If you travel too long without your body, your heartbeat will stop and you will die.

Ingredients

1 lavender full flower (including the roots)
2 mint leaves
1 teaspoon of soul flower seeds
1/4 tablespoon of crushed spirit crystal
1/4 cup of orchid petals
1/4 cup of lily petal

Instructions

Bring to boil in two cups of water the lavender, mint, soul flower seeds, orchid petals, and lily petals.
Crush the spirit crystal into a powder.
Add the crystal powder to the mix.
Drink the full mix slowly, like a hot chocolate.
Eat the remaining of the flowers.
Lie down and try to sleep.

Your heartbeat will slow drastically. When you feel lightheaded, focus on your spirit and order it to ascend to the place desired. A little part of your soul will remain in your body. The rest will float out of your body. It is imperative that you listen to the whole you, including the little piece of soul left in your body. If there is a danger or a crisis, you are to return immediately into your body; otherwise, you will die. When you feel the serum wear off, you will have thirty seconds to go back into your body; otherwise, you will die.

"Miss Pomegrade, do we have crystals on this island" I asked.

"We certainly do. Why?"

"Just wondering. Where can I find them?"

"It depends on which one you are looking for."

"How about the spirit crystal?"

"This is an extremely rare stone found mostly in South Africa. I have a collection of crystals from all over the world. We have a crystal shop here open on the weekends. Mr. Gemstone searches for them all over the world and brings them back here."

"How do we pay for it?"

"We don't pay. It works the same way as the ring store. If one crystal is meant to be yours, it will rotate on its own when your ring points at it. It means it's yours to keep. Most people return empty-handed. They say there a spirit inside all crystals that can read people's minds and they will know if you need something."

"Cool! The store will be open tomorrow then?"

"Yes."

"Where will it be?"

"It will be in the flea market right in front of the cafeteria."

"What else is there at the flea market?"

"Flowers, a tattoo shop, roots shop, clothing shop, jewelry, books, junk, etc."

"Cool."

Students started to come back with the herbs. I closed my book and hid it in my bag before anyone could see it.

＊ ＊ ＊ ＊ ＊

At the Teleportation School, Miss Travel sent a little group of students with me so I could teach them how to teleport form one corner to the other while she was working with the ones who were still trying to move things around. Apparently, Master Thunderstone didn't allow me to be excused from any school. By the end of the school, two students, Bella and Kaden, were able to teleport from one corner to the other. They were very excited, and they thanked me. They said they had both tried for two weeks but had never managed to teleport before that day. Miss Travel was surprised; she didn't expect that. She almost seemed offended that they succeeded without her guiding them.

* * * * *

Everybody was around the ring. Mr. Corrigan picked two names: Mel and Christian. The fighting was on, and I analyzed their every move, but it made me nervous. I'd never fought for real before. I didn't want to hurt anyone, and I didn't want to get hurt, especially not today. I had an important mission to do later. I would need all my strength. Mel won on the third round. It was a fairly easy win. His face was still intact; on the other hand, Christian's face was pretty swollen around his left eye, and his lower lip was bleeding.

Mr. Corrigan picked two more names: Ashley and Joshua. "Great!" I thought. I put my gloves on and went to the middle of the ring. Mr. Corrigan looked at me and said telepathically, "Just remember to dance. You got this." I looked at him and tried a faint smile. I'm sure it was barely visible.

I could hear Joshua's thoughts. "A beginner girl...piece of cake. I'll give her one round. I'll try not to hit her beautiful face. She's too pretty to fight." The first round I just danced, avoiding the hits, listening to his mind. Right before the second round, Mr. Corrigan looked at me and said in front of everyone, "You'd better start throwing some punches, Ashley. It's not a dance contest." Everybody laughed at his comment. I looked at him with defeated eyes. In the second round, I managed to give Joshua a few light punches in the ribs, but he didn't seem to feel it. I heard Mr. Corrigan say telepathically, "Come on, Ashley. Pretend Joshua is the murderer that is going to kill a loved one." Joshua was trying to provoke me by doing the "Come on, bring it on" move with his glove. I read his mind. I knew he was going to punch me on the left side of my face. I moved to the right, avoided his hit, and punched him hard in his right ribs. He didn't see that one coming. That one hurt him bad enough that he was out of breath for a few seconds. I jabbed him in the jaw. He fell on the ground. He had ten seconds to get up before he would lose the fight. At the count of ten, Mr. Corrigan blew the whistle, and I won. When I got out, Veronica gave me a dirty look. Mel and Julius gave me a high five.

I looked for Veronica; she was avoiding my looks. She was mad at me for hitting Joshua and winning the fight. "But what was I supposed to do? Let him hit me and lose on purpose?" I thought to myself.

At the end of the school, both Veronica and Stephany left school without looking at me or speaking to me. They rushed out of school, and Julius and Mel tagged along with them. I was left alone, which I needed to be at that time, although I felt rejected and unwanted again. I waited for everybody to be gone, and I teleported to the Grounding School. Miss Pomegrade was waiting for me, and she had a very nervous look on her face.

"Now make sure to drink enough for forty-five minutes, just to be on the safe side," she said.

"I know, I know. Let's just hope Miss Grace will be there in time to let me out," I replied.

"Quick, I see them coming. They are early!"

I drank the duplicate serum, picturing a beautiful butterfly in my head. My entire body ached, and I felt very dizzy. When I heard footsteps coming on the front porch, I transformed into a butterfly just in time. The sensation was indescribable. I felt as light as a feather and as fragile as an egg without bones. I felt sticky: my hard cuticles were coated with wax, simi-lar to beeswax. I was tempted to try my wings, but there was no time to experiment. Miss Pomegrade gently put me in the little black case. It was so dark in there I couldn't see anything, I felt claustrophobic. I couldn't breathe properly due to the lack of oxygen in the case. I heard some voices, but it was hard to distinguish what was said because everything sounded so muddled. I knew we were moving, and after a while, the motion made me feel sick. It's seemed like the longest ride of my life.

Just when I felt weak and lightheaded enough to faint, somebody opened the case. The light that shone in was blinding, but I was thankful for the oxygen. I was tempted to fly out and free myself, but I remembered my mission. I had to spy without being seen. I saw a big hand reaching down for the tarantula venom. It almost touched me, and I had to step into the corner of the bag to stay hidden. I counted to five and decided to risk taking a peek. I saw a man with the flask in his hand. I didn't have a clear view from there. I had to take a chance. I flew out.

It felt great to spread my wings, but now was not the time. On a desk I could read the sign "Mr. Blake." So Mr. Corrigan was right. I was in his office. Like he had predicted, Mr. Blake was walking toward a safe. It was a huge safe, the size of a big fridge. I had to see the code. I gently and carefully landed on his head. I had a great view from there. I saw the code: 23-37-64. I memorized it. When he opened the safe, inside were hundreds of labeled flasks. There were five shelves. The top one was full of venoms from different insects and snakes. The two last shelves had no names, just numbers: 392 and 393. I immediately understood what it meant: the number of the pages where the blank pages of the lethal serum and the serum of destruction were inserted. I couldn't believe it!

I focused and tried to read his mind: "I'm so hungry. What time is it?" he asked himself as he looked at his watch. It was 5:15. "It's just about time to go to the cafeteria. Maybe I should call it a day. Wow, the backup sure is getting full. Good thing we will be able to use it soon. The plant is just about ready. I can't wait to test it on humans. I think I'll start with the United States first, where it would hurt the most. Their time is up."

Mr. Blake closed and locked the safe and gathered his things. He was ready to leave. I looked at the time: 5:20. I still had time to explore and look around for cameras or a security system. He had mentioned this was not the only backup. Where would the rest be? I decided to stay on his head and spy from there. It was safer this way. He was in the hallway when his cellphone rang. I took a few steps closer to his ear.

"Hello, Master, what can I do for you?"

"Are we clear to talk?"

"Yes, I'm alone."

"How are we in stock?"

"Good. Why?"

"Do we have enough to experiment on a city?"

"Yes. What city did you have in mind?"

"I was thinking Washington, D.C. The White House is getting too confident and powerful in the world. We need to correct this and remind them that they are not invincible."

"It shouldn't be a problem, sir. Did you have a date in mind?"

"I was thinking two weeks from today, April 27."

"How many gallons should we use?"

"How many do we have in total?"

"Twenty gallons, plus half a gallon in backup."

"I think one gallon should be enough for a city. What do you think.

"I guess we'll find out for sure on the twenty-seventh."

"Good. Let's keep this one quiet for now. I want you to pick a partner for this mission, and I want you in the field."

"Yes, sir."

He continued to walk and stopped at the elevator. Then he stepped inside with three other men, all going to the main floor.

"Hey, Mr. Blake, I heard you got another sample of tarantula venom today."

"Yes, fancy that."

"With that sample, we will be able to make, what? Two more gallons?"

"If not three."

"Good gracious. Got to love them; they are so ugly, but they sure are useful."

"You got that right."

"Hey, what do you make out of this new girl...Ashley? You think we should eliminate her?"

"Eliminate her? No, not now. She's just a smart one; you know what I mean. We could use her brain, if we could get her on our side. Let's just keep an eye on her for now."

"So you don't think she's a threat?"

"I think she's more of an asset than a threat. She's just a young pup. With her brain, she would be more useful here than any other domain. She could be our new lethal weapon."

Mr. Blake scratched his head and almost crushed me. I discretely fluttered away and climbed the elevator's wall. They all walked out of the elevator. Time was running out. I had to get to the front door, but I didn't know which way to go. I fluttered close behind Mr. Blake while he was walking toward security. He had to scan his briefcase and walk through security, empty-handed. I decided it was a good time to quickly fly away. I saw the door from where I was, and I flew in that direction. I could hear Miss Grace's voice; she was talking louder than normal to a man, clearly trying to stall.

"Oh, excuse me, I have a call coming. I need to take this." She walked back a few steps toward the front door, pretending to talk on the phone. I could see she was looking for me. I heard her mind scream, "Come on, Ashley! Where are you? Time is running out! It's 5:32. I can't wait here indefinitely. He will start to get suspicious!"

"I'm coming, I'm coming! To your left. Pretend you need to leave. Hurry!" I screamed back.

"Oh, I'm sorry, Jason. Something came up, and I need to go. Should we take a rain check?"

"Sure, how about tomorrow?"

"OK, I will try, but I can't promise anything."

When she saw me, she opened the door, blew him a kiss, and stepped out.

I quickly said thanks to Miss Grace and flew away. I knew she deserved an explanation; I just needed time to myself. It was just too much to take in right now. Flying in the sky felt good. I knew I didn't have much time left as a butterfly, but I wanted to fly until I couldn't anymore. I was tempted to go in the forbidden forest, but I knew I didn't have enough time. I flew toward the Grounding School, on top of the hill. A few students were still there. I was tempted to go spy on them, but my wings were getting stiffer.

As I reached the porch, I felt dizzy, and my body ached. I landed on the window. When Miss Pomegrade saw me, she let me in. I transformed into Ashley shortly afterward.

"Thank goodness, Ashley. I was so worried. Here, take this glass of water. You look awful."

I took the glass and drank the water all at once.

"Did you find out anything useful?"

"Yes, but let's have a meeting tonight, same place, same time. I need to get to the cafeteria before they notice my absence," I replied.

When I entered the cafeteria, Mr. Corrigan looked at me. He clearly looked worried, but when I gave him the thumbs–up, he calmed down. I went to my table. Veronica made sure there was no space available beside her or her friends. I had no energy left. I took a seat on the other side of the table, alone. When I sat down, I collapsed on the floor unconscious.

I was floating toward the light. The stars were guiding me. Someone was waiting for me. As I was approaching my soul group, one soul in particular stood out. He was giving me a high five. Although he didn't look the same, he stood tall in the bright light, and I knew it was my old soul friend, Victor, from many past lives. He teased me, saying, "Well, it took you long enough to figure it out! I guess it's better late than never!"

"Well, who is doing all the dirty work again? You? Try to be in this body and live my life and see if you can do better than me!" I replied.

"Ashley! Ashley!" said a familiar voice. I felt cold water on my forehead.

"Oh, oh! Time's up! You'd better go back and finish this," said Victor.

"I don't want to. I want to stay with you, with all of you. I'm tired of this life."

"Well, you signed up for this, remember? You knew it was going to be tough. Now go on."

I flew back fast; my body was pulling me back. When I re-entered my body, I was in Mr. Corrigan arms, surrounded by familiar faces. Veronica was among them. She was holding my hand. My mouth was so dry that my throat hurt.

"What happened?" was all I managed to say.

"You fainted, collapsed on the floor," replied Mr. Corrigan. His eyes met mine, and I could tell he was worried. "Give her space. She needs to rest."

I lifted my head and said, "I'm fine. Just tired, that's all."

His mind said, "No, you are not, Ashley. I should never have agreed to this..." but his voice said, "Take it easy. How is your head?"

"OK. I'm OK," I said out loud. But I told him telepathically, "It was a great idea. Wait until you learn what I found out. I told the others to meet tonight, same place, same time." He nodded and helped me sit down at the table.

"Maybe she just needs to eat. I'll go make her a plate," said Veronica.

After eating, my energy started to return. "Thanks, Veronica. I'm sorry about Joshua. I didn't mean to upset you....I..."

"Don't mention it. You had no choice. I get that now."

* * * * *

I teleported to the Warriors School at 8:57 p.m. Miss Grace, Miss Pomegrade, and Mr. Corrigan got up.

"I heard you gave quite a scare to everyone tonight," said Miss Pomegrade.

"Yes, she managed to get everybody's attention again, and that's the last thing we need," said Mr. Corrigan.

"Yeah, well, you try to transform into a tarantula and then a butterfly on the same day and see how you feel after," I replied.

"So what did you find out? Was it worth it?" asked Miss Grace.

"Oh, that they already have twenty gallons of the serum of destruction, and I don't know how many gallons of the lethal serum, plus a good backup in Mr. Blake's safe. Yes, you were right, but that's only the backup. And get this—they plan on testing the serum of destruction on Washington, D.C., on April 27."

"What? But that's in two weeks!" said Miss Pomegrade.

"How do you know this?" asked Miss Grace.

"It's incredible what you can find out when you spy as a butterfly. It was Master Thunderstone's orders. I heard their whole conversation on the phone."

"How did you manage that?" asked Miss Pomegrade.

"I was hiding on his head."

"You are crazy," said Miss Grace, laughing.

"I don't see how this is funny. This is serious. We need to come up with a plan and stop this from happening," said Mr. Corrigan.

"Anything else we should know about?" asked Miss Pomegrade.

"No. Well, maybe. Some people want me dead."

"Well, that's not surprising," said Mr. Corrigan.

"Gee, thanks."

"You are new, an outsider, and threatening. Someone who keeps getting all the attention when you should be keeping a low profile; you are an easy target," said Mr. Corrigan. "But we have bigger problems than this. How can we stop them?" he said coldly.

That response somehow hurt me, but I tried to push away the feeling. It felt as though he didn't care if I were killed.

"Well, we need to destroy the serum," I said, trying to hide my disappointment.

"Yes, but how?" asked Mr. Corrigan.

"By finding the factory. It's somewhere on this island."

"And how are we supposed to find it? By changing into butterflies, waiting for birds to eat us? That won't work!" said Mr. Corrigan.

"By spying. They will be working overtime now that the date is approaching. We could try to follow them."

"Yes, why don't I just put on my invisible mask?" said Mr. Corrigan.

"What's with the attitude tonight?" asked Miss Grace.

"Wait! That gives me an idea. What if I could make an invisible serum?" I proposed.

"And how would you do that? You think you can just invent one?" asked Mr. Corrigan.

"Yes."

"With what? How?"

"By using my brain and the formula volume. I'm not saying I will succeed, but I'll give it a shot. Admit it. It would be great if we could all be invisible for a while."

"You're dreaming, girl, if you ever think that would work," said Miss Grace.

"Unless you want to change with me into a bird or a butterfly, I don't think we have much of a choice," I said.

"I'll pass, thank you," she answered.

"You're all chicken shits," I teased.

"Why don't we call it a night? Ashley, you need to rest. You've done more than enough today. We learned a lot, thanks to you, but we'll all think more clearly after some sleep. It was a stressful day, and I am ready for bed. Why don't we meet tomorrow night, same time?" suggested Miss Pomegrade.

"Fine by me!" said the two other teachers. All eyes fell on me, waiting for my answer.

"OK. I should have a recipe by tomorrow night," I said.

"How can you be so sure of yourself?" asked Mr. Corrigan.

"I am not. But what good will it do if we don't try?" I said.

"OK, have a good night. I'm gonna head home," said Miss Grace before she teleported home.

"I'm off too. See you tomorrow!" said Miss Pomegrade.

Mr. Corrigan and I were alone, looking awkwardly at each other. His eyes met mine.

"What's wrong? Did I do something wrong?" I asked him.

"No, why?"

"Then why are you so angry with me?"

"What are you talking about? Go home. You are tired, and you are speaking nonsense"

I looked him straight in the eyes. I could read his mind. I could see he was jealous. He was used to being the brilliant one with all the ideas—that was, until I came along. He was annoyed that I came up with all different kinds of ideas and that I saved the day, and most of all, that I was just a student. He didn't like to be second best. He was used to being the champion. He felt like he didn't do anything useful today, and he didn't like that. He liked to be in charge, not to being told what to do, and I understood where he was coming from, so I decided to leave him alone and not make things worse.

"OK. Good night, Mr. Corrigan," I said. Then I teleported to my room.

CHAPTER ELEVEN

I woke up at 10 the next morning. I had worked until late in the night to find a recipe to make the invisible serum, and after a while, I did. I couldn't be sure until I tested it though. Today my plan was to go to the market to find what I needed. And find Miss Pomegrade so she could give me certain ingredients.

I got up, took a long shower, and put on an old pair of jeans and tank top. I had no school today, so I assumed I didn't have to dress in school clothing. When I went to the cafeteria, only a few students were there. I was the only one at my table when Mr. Corrigan walked in. I decided not to pay him any attention, to keep my distance from him, even if he was hard to resist. He was talking with other adults, not even acknowledging me, so I had my breakfast and left.

I went to the flea market. It was much bigger than I thought it would be. It was full of people, mostly adults. There were lots of strangers and families with younger kids and babies, but not many students. I guessed it was not the thing to do here. I wondered where all the students were, where they hung out on the weekend. Antoinette crossed my mind, as she had many times this week, and I wished she were with me. We used to have so much fun together. Today I felt alone. You would think I would be used to it by now, but I never was. After three hours at the flea market, my hands were full, and I brought the bags to my room. I had found most of the ingredients that I needed. Then I returned to the flea market. There was a specific crystal that I was looking for: the spirit quartz. I was happy to find some—or should I say, it found me. It started spinning as soon as I walked in. The saleswoman wrapped it for me, and as I was walking out, Miss Pomegrade walked in.

"It's nice to see you here," said Miss Pomegrade.

"Yes, I was hoping to see you actually."

"Oh yeah, why?"

"Because I am missing one ingredient in particular for my serum, and I was hoping you would have some, or at least know where to get it," I whispered.

"Oh yeah, which one is that?"

"*Daucus Carota* with a deep purple fairy seed in the middle."

"They are extremely rare, but it just so happens that I have one in my private flowerbed."

"Do you think I could use it?" I asked.

"Well, are you sure it's what you need? I mean it is one of a kind, and I would hate to waste it."

"I can't guarantee without trying it."

"Oh...well...I guess so, but right now, only I have access to it. Give me a few minutes. I'll go get it and come right back. Don't leave," she said before she disappeared.

While waiting, I saw Seth and Mr. Corrigan in the sword shop. They were admiring one sword in particular. I could almost swear they were best friends, they seemed to get along so well. Mr. Corrigan sensed me watching him and turned to look at me. He held my glare for just a little too long. Seth notice Mr. Corrigan's stare, and he followed his glare; his eyes fell on me. At the sight of me, he tensed up. I could hear his thoughts as he said to Mr. Corrigan, "I swear there is something odd with that girl. She gives me the creeps. I don't trust her."

"She's definitely different. I don't know what to make of her," said Mr. Corrigan.

"You watch, she will be nothing but trouble. Many people want her dead, you know. I knew I should have killed her when I had the chance."

"Yeah, well, you know the rules here. You can't eliminate her until she's proven guilty."

"There is always something to be guilty for."

Mr. Corrigan didn't reply. I'd heard enough, and I walked away from them. Miss Pomegrade came back shortly after with a little bag. She gave it to me. I could see from the corner of my eyes Mr. Corrigan watching.

"Thanks, Miss Pomegrade. Hey, do you trust Mr. Corrigan?"

"Of course. Why?"

"He just acts...suspiciously sometimes."

"He is unfriendly by nature, and sometimes he can be odd, I'll admit, but don't worry; he is on our side, even if he acts differently in front of the others. It's just an act."

"OK, thanks. I'll see you tonight?"

"Yes, good luck."

* * * * *

Later in the afternoon when it was pouring rain, I decided to go train at the Warriors School. A few students were there from the Warriors Devotion House, and they looked at me like I didn't belong there.

"What are you doing here? Go play somewhere else, you freak," said Steven.

"I won't bother you. I just wanted to train, that's all."

"Get out. This is our place to hang around, and you aren't invited," said Steven.

"Don't worry. I am not here to hang out with you guys." At that, I walked straight to the shooting range, away from them. They were shouting things at me, but I didn't care. I didn't even look at them. I sucked at my first ten shots, but after a while, I started to get better. Steven and his bunch came to show off in front of me. They could all hit the middle target. I didn't say anything; instead I went running on the track. After my first round, they came sprinting ahead of me calling out, "Slow poke" while passing me. On the second turn around, they bumped into me, making me fall to the ground.

"Oops!" they said, laughing.

On the third round, they grabbed me by the arms, and Steven started to punch me in the face and ribs. The other four boys held me still, all of them laughing out loud. Steven punched me like a mad man. He was going to kill me. I knew what moves he was going to do before he would hit me, but I couldn't defend myself without the use of my arms and my legs. I was trapped; there was nothing I could do. My mouth and face were bleeding, and I knew I had at least two broken ribs. I was in so much pain, and I was losing so much blood. I thought it was the end of me. I thought for sure I was going to die. The only thing that was left to do was to try to call for help telepathically. I screamed for help to Mr. Corrigan and Miss Grace. I didn't hear any response. I was fading away; my vision blurred and then things started going black. All of a sudden, I heard a shout from afar. The boys let me go and ran. I fell to the ground and tried to open my eyes, but they were swollen shut. I heard somebody run, and then everything went black.

CHAPTER TWELVE

A beam of light called me.

"My dear child, what are you doing here again? It is not your time. I didn't send you to Earth for you to end like this."

"There was nothing I could do. They attacked in a group from behind."

"Why were you there in the first place? You shouldn't have been there. You should know better. When they started bullying you, why didn't you walk away?"

"I wasn't about to let them walk all over me."

"Ah! Pride can be a good thing to stay strong, and you need to be for this mission. But, my child, you need to be alert and on your toes at all times. If it means embarrassment, so be it, if it's for the better. The world relies on your safety and integrity."

"Father, I failed my mission. I'll try to do better in my next life."

"Your presence in this life is not finished yet. You have the power to go back."

"I can't go back. I have no energy left...and I have no desire to go back to her body. I didn't choose well. I thought it would be easier to have all these powers and intelligence, but look where it brought me...right back here. Mission failed."

"I sent you for this mission precisely because you had the powers and intelligence to succeed. Go back and finish it. You know where you can find your energy. Focus."

I closed my eyes and breathed in my father's energy and focus on my heart. I saw a bright white light coming out of my heart. I forgave Steven and his friends for bullying and attacking me. I suddenly felt a heat going through my veins, and then I felt a heartbeat.

"Ashley! Ashley, hang in there!" Someone was pouring cold water on my face. "You are safe with me now. Can you hear me? Please...give me a sign. Please, Ashley...focus...focus on my voice. I need to know you will be OK. If you can hear me, squeeze my hand."

I tried. I squeeze faintly. I wasn't sure he felt it.

"Oh, thank God! Ashley, you need to focus on healing yourself, just like you did the other day. Do your magic," said Mr. Corrigan.

He was patting my head and holding my hand. I could feel ice packs on my head and my ribs. I wanted to open my eyes, but they were too swollen. I tried to say something, but my jaw was in so much pain, I couldn't move it.

"Come on, Ash, I know you can do it. I have faith in you. I can't lose you now. I'm sorry I was a jerk earlier."

I could feel his hand on mine. When he started rubbing my hand with his thumb, the friction gave me energy. I suddenly wanted desperately to open my eyes and look into his. I started to focus on my eyes, asking my mind to heal them.

"That's it! That's it, Ashley. Keep focusing. It's working! Wow! That's incredible!"

I opened my eyes. His eyes met mine.

"Hey, you! Welcome back! Keep working. You are not done yet. You still look pretty beat up," he teased me.

I wanted to smile, but I couldn't. My jaw was broken. I focused on my jaw, then on my ribs, then the rest of my face. Within half an hour, I was as good as new.

"Thanks," I managed to say.

"No thanks required. You did most of the work. I just brought you here and tried to clean your wounds."

"Do I still look beat up?"

"No, you are as pretty as ever. Not a scratch." He was embarrassed to say that out loud; he'd said it without thinking.

"Where am I anyway?"

"I teleported you to my private suite. I didn't want to bring you to the hospital—that would attract too much attention, and attention is the last thing you want. Beside, you would have been stuck there for days before they would release you, and time is not something we have. I knew you could heal yourself."

"Wow! Look at my favorite shirt! It's ruined. I must have lost a lot of blood!"

"You certainly did. You were unconscious for a while...I was afraid to lose you. That's twice now. Don't make this a habit. Here, take this shirt. You can't walk around with that bloody shirt on. Why don't you go take a shower? Your hair is covered in blood. Take your time. I have a few things to do, and I'll be right back."

"Thanks, Mr. Corrigan."

"When it's just the two of us, you can call me Collin."

"Thanks, Collin," I said with a smile.

He gave me a towel. The shower felt good. I had no clue how long I had been unconscious, and I had no clue what time it was. When I came out of the shower and got dressed, the first thing I asked Collin for was the time.

"6:05 p.m."

"What? I'm so sorry, Collin. You'd better go to the buffet before it closes."

"It's Saturday night. Not many people go to the buffet. Most people go out for dinner."

"Go out where? We are stuck on this island."

"We go to the Live Night Street. It's open only on the weekends."

"Really? Where is it?"

"Here, I have something for you. Get dressed in this, and I'll show you. Sorry about the disguise, I just thought you'd look older in this. We can't afford to be seen together. Unless you want to go hang out with your friends. I'm sure they are in the teens club."

"No, I don't fit in with them, and I really don't want to see Steven and his friends."

"That's what I thought. It's safer to stay away from him for a while. Go on, try it on. I didn't know your size, but I took a guess."

I couldn't believe it. It was a fitted black dress with high heels and a chin-length red wig. He even got lipstick for me. It all fit me like a glove. I really did look older. I couldn't stop looking at myself in the mirror. I was stunning. I didn't think I would like the wig, but it looked good. It brought out my blue eyes. I had a hard time walking in the high shoes.

"Where are we going anyway?" I asked, but my appearance distracted him and he took a while to respond. He was admiring me.

"You look beautiful!" was all he managed to say.

"Thanks. What should my name be tonight?"

"You pick one."

"Antoinette."

"Antoinette it is."

"And who am I supposed to be?"

"I'm not sure. Let me do the talking. I'll figure something out," said Collin.

"Won't people be curious to see you with a stranger?"

"They will be very curious. Let's just say you are a spy from the outside world."

"And why would I be with you?"

Mélanie C. Larue   124

"Let's just say you are trying to recruit me for a job. That will be convincing enough."

"Where are we going?"

"Give me your hand. I'll teleport you there."

"What about our meeting tonight?" I asked.

"I canceled it. I rescheduled for tomorrow," he answered.

He took my hand, and we teleported to the Live Night Street. I couldn't believe my eyes. Everything was lit. It reminded me of Las Vegas. There were people everywhere, line-ups everywhere, including street performers and live bands.

"Wow!" was all I could say.

"Are you hungry?"

"Starving."

CHAPTER THIRTEEN

We walked in front of the Teens Club, and from what I could see, it was packed and wild. Steven was smoking outside with his friends. He looked at me and whistled; it made the hair on the back of my neck stand up. When he realized I was with Mr. Corrigan, he said, "Oh, sorry, Mr. Corrigan. I didn't realize it was you. Nice evening, ey?"

Collin ignored him. He took my hand and said, "Are you OK?"

"He gives me the creeps, but it was obvious he didn't recognize me," I said.

We continued walking and saw Miss Grace with a man; they were double-dating with Seth and his date. She stopped and asked, "Hey, Collin, what are you doing here? And who might this be?"

"Hi, Grace." He politely nodded to the others. "Going to grab a bite to eat. This is...Antoinette. Antoinette, this is Grace, Martin, Seth, and Kaitlyn."

Everybody watched me curiously.

"You want to join us? We are going to the Wizards Club."

"No, I think we'll pass. We'd like to go somewhere quieter."

"Gotcha," she said with a big smile. She gave him a wink.

We went to a little Mexican club, and we chose a table in a secluded corner.

"What are the chances of seeing them? Now she will have ten thousand questions that I'll have to answer about you."

I laughed. The server came to greet us.

"What can I get you two lovebirds? Would you like to try our house wine?"

I blushed. He kept his cool.

"Um, sure."

When the server left, he said, "You can have a glass. If you don't like it, I'll drink it."

The server came back with two glasses. I tasted the wine but didn't like it. I must have made a face because Collin said, "It's a taste you will develop in time. You don't have to drink it. Here, have some water."

After a few sips of the wine, it tasted less bitter.

"Did I tell you I created the serum we talked about last night?"

"Really? Does it work?"

"I didn't have a chance to test it yet. I wanted to do that tonight."

"Tomorrow will have to do, I guess," Collin reassured me.

We had a pleasant night. We laughed a lot. We talked about our child-hoods and the Ancestral School. It felt good to talk to someone who was similar to me. Next thing we knew, it was past 11 p.m., and a live band was playing. Collin's eyes were so bright, I couldn't stop looking at him. We had finished the whole bottle of wine, and some people were dancing. He asked me to dance.

"I told you, I can't dance."

"Just follow my steps and dance, kind of like we did in the ring."

He took my hand and led me to the dance floor. His touch was electrifying, and he held me close. My heartbeat quickened when I felt his breath on my neck. I felt awkward on the dance floor.

"Just follow my steps, Ash. There you go. See, you're doing so well."

We finished the dance, and then a second song came on,—"All of Me" by John Legend—and we stayed for this one too. It came more naturally the second time around. I was starting to enjoy dancing with him. He looked into my eyes, and I held his gaze for what seemed like an eternity. He slowly leaned down and kissed me. It was a soft, tender, and brief kiss on my lips, and it gave me butterflies. When he saw that I didn't pull away, he kissed me longer for a second time. He tasted like wine and fajitas. We kissed for a long time and pulled away only when the song was over.

"Sorry, you two lovebirds. It's closing time."

We left, laughing and holding hands.

"It's past midnight. We should head back home," said Collin. I nodded.

"Thanks, Collin, I had a great time. In fact, I don't remember the last time I had this much fun."

"Same. Can you keep...whatever this is between us a secret?"

"Don't worry. My lips are sealed."

"You know, I can't play favoritism with you at school."

"I know. You're the teacher. I'm just a student."

"You are not just a student to me, but nobody needs to know that."

He smiled at me.

"There's just one more thing I need to do before we teleport back to our respective rooms," said Collin.

He put his hand on my face, and then he kissed me passionately.

"We'd better stop now or I won't be able to let you go," he said. I smiled, and then we left.

CHAPTER FOURTEEN

I teleported to the Warriors School at 8:55 p.m., as scheduled. Miss Pomegrade was already there, talking to Collin, but there was no sign of Miss Grace yet.

"Good evening, Ashley" said Miss Pomegrade. "Mr. Corrigan just told me what happened yesterday."

I blushed and looked at Collin questioningly.

"That Steven and his friends beat you almost to death, and what condition you were in when I found you," he said.

"Right." Silly me, I thought to myself, I had totally forgotten about that. I thought he was referring to our evening together.

"It's hard to believe. You look exactly the same as before," she said. "Wait until he sees you. He's going to be shocked."

"Yeah, what am I supposed to say to him?"

"You don't say anything. He will be afraid of you. It's not like he is going to report what he did, so he will always wonder how you did it," said Collin. He looked at me, and when Miss Pomegrade wasn't looking, he winked at me. I smiled back. I had been waiting all day to see him, and he gave me butterflies every time I looked his way. Miss Grace came in with a smile on her face.

"Well, hello there, Mr. Corrigan! Did you have fun last night?" she asked.

He tried to avoid the question by saying, "It looks like you certainly did."

"Did I miss something here?" asked Miss Pomegrade.

"Yes, Collin had a hot date last night!"

"It wasn't a date. It was a business meeting."

"Right!"

"It's true!"

"Oh really? What kind of business then?"

"Top secret. I can't tell you."

"May I remind you guys that we are in presence of a student," said Miss Pomegrade.

They both dropped the subject and looked at me.

"Sorry, Ashley. Did you manage to create the serum?" asked Miss Grace.

"Yes. I would like to test it in front of you guys, if you don't mind."

"Be my guest," Miss Grace said.

I drank the serum. I immediately felt a tingling sensation in my hands and feet, and then my whole body felt numb. My hands disappeared, then my arms, and soon after, so did everything else.

"Wow! That's amazing, Ashley!" said Miss Pomegrade.

"Can you hear us?" asked Collin.

"Yes," I replied.

"Way to go, Ashley!" said Collin, doing a high five. I hit his hand; he didn't see it coming. He started laughing.

"Now we have to count how many minutes it will last," I said.

"Good point. We can't go spy like this without knowing the time frame we have," said Collin.

"This is huge, Ashley. Imagine what we could do if it works long enough!" said Miss Grace.

"Now someone should drink double the amount to compare the time frame," I suggested.

"I'll do it," said Collin.

He drank a cup of the serum. First, his head was flicking like a weak light bulb, then his torso. Within thirty seconds, he was totally invisible.

"Can you see me?" he asked.

"No," said both the teachers.

"I can," I said.

"I can see you too, Ashley," he said. He smiled at me and waved me over. I came closer to him, and he kissed me. I pulled back quickly. He said to me telepathically, "Relax, they can't see us."

"Right," I replied, so I kissed him this time.

"Well, while we wait, why don't you tell us about your hot date, Collin."

I decided to play along.

"What, Mr. Corrigan had a hot date last night?" I said.

Collin looked at me with warning eyes. I smiled at him.

"Yes, he did. Well, aren't you going to tell us?"

"Tell you what? There is nothing to say. I told you, it wasn't a date."

"Are you saying she wasn't hot?" I asked, still teasing him.

"No, she was. She's a very attractive woman, but it wasn't a date." And then he told me telepathically "OK, satisfied? Now drop it."

"Well, are you going to see her again?" asked Miss Pomegrade.

"I don't know...maybe."

After half an hour of bullshitting, I became visible again; and after an hour, Collin became visible. We took note that half a cup gave us half an hour of invisibility and a full cup gave us an hour. It was already late, so we decided to use the serum the next day at 9 p.m. Same meeting point.

* * * * *

When Steven saw me at the cafeteria Monday morning, his mouth dropped. He elbowed his friends; they were all looking at me like I was a ghost. I purposely walked by them and dared to say out loud, "What's the matter? You look like you've seen a ghost! Or has the cat got your tongue?"

They didn't reply; they simply stared at me. The day started out great. I managed to clear seven more lives, although I apparently still struggled with one particular memory, and then I completed the sleeping serum within five minutes once again. I was free to go. With forty-five minutes to waste, I decided to take half a cup of the invisible serum and go explore the forbidden places around the beach. No crows or flies could see me this time...no butterflies either. All of a sudden, I heard a loud roar ahead of me, then a loud high-pitched scream. I wondered where it was coming from because, whatever it was, it didn't sound good. A few minutes later, two men appeared out of nowhere. "They must have teleported," I thought. I was terrified to see that one man was bleeding a lot. Part of his left arm was missing. They passed right beside me.

"Hang on, Corey. We made it through the protective shield. You are safe here. I will teleport us to the hospital."

And they were gone again. Now I was more curious than ever. I took note of where they appeared in front of me. It must be some sort of secret portal access to the forbidden place. I looked at my watch. I only had twenty minutes left. I placed an X with two sticks where I was and decided to look on the other side. I focused on the portal and tried to cross to the other side of the shield. It worked. I was now on the beach. At first I thought I was alone, but then I saw people running right and left, alarmed. One man was severely burned on the right side of his face. He was holding on to someone, screaming and heading toward the portal. I looked to my right. I saw people coming out of what looked like a hill and some kind of camouflage building. When the door was closed, you would never guess it was there. *This must be it!* I looked at my watch. It was time to head back before the serum faded away. I was about to turn around when I saw two men running out of the hill with guns, heading for behind the bush. *There must be something there, hidden in the bush.* Again, I heard a big roar followed by gunshots. I was curious and wanted to check it out, but I didn't have enough time. I ran back to the portal and teleported into the cafeteria.

I wanted to talk to Mr. Corrigan and let him know what I'd seen. But the first person I saw was my favorite person in the whole world: Steven. The sight of him got my mind side-tracked. I'm not sure exactly what made me do it. Maybe it was my way of getting even. I had the uncontrollable urge to make fun of him or scare him. I took advantage of the fact that I was still invisible and walked by him and made him drop his tray of food on the floor, and then I took his hat and threw it like a Frisbee across the cafeteria. He looked stunned. I didn't stop there. I dared to pull his pants down to his knees. Everybody was laughing and pointing at him. I then whispered in his ear, "I know what you did to Ashley. Leave her alone or you will deal with me."

He was so freaked out that he ran out of the cafeteria. His friends were clueless about what was going on. They just stood there, not knowing what to do. I took advantage of the situation and tied their shoelaces together. Steven popped his head back in the cafeteria and motioned for his friends to follow him. They tried to obey, but when they took their first steps, they tripped and fell to the floor, dropping their trays of food too.

I saw Collin coming toward them, angry. "What's going on here? Clean up this mess! Hey, Steven, come here." Steven came running to him. "Clean this up! If I ever catch you pulling your pants down in a public place ever again, you will be suspended for a week. Do you hear me?"

"But sir...I didn't do it...It was..."

"I don't want to hear it, Steven. Now pick it up!"

I had to put my hand to my mouth to hide my laughter. I started to feel the serum effect fade away, so I ran for the entrance. When I walked back into the cafeteria, I was visible. Steven and his friends were still picking up their mess. I walked by them. They all stopped and looked at me.

"Hey, Ashley! I need to talk to you," Steven whispered.

"I have no desire to speak with you," I replied and walked away.

Collin was serving himself. I went to join him before finding a place to sit. I asked him telepathically, "You want to join me for a jog after lunch? I discovered something new."

"Sorry, Ash, I can't. I have a meeting right after. Is everything OK?" he thought.

"Yes."

"I'll see you later then."

And he left me alone. I served myself and sat down at my table.

"There you are! Where were you hiding all this time? I can never find you!" said Veronica

"I wasn't hiding."

"Where were you then?"

"I went for a walk, that's all."

"Where were you this weekend? I looked all over for you. I wanted to bring you to the Teens Club."

"I was sick all weekend. I stayed in my bedroom most of the time."

"That's sucks," said Julius.

"Are you getting excited for this coming weekend?" asked Veronica.

"What's happening this weekend?"

"The dance!"

"Well, I am excited for the tournament, but not for the dance."

"What is wrong with you? It's your chance to meet the guy of your dreams and to wear a pretty dress."

"I don't have any dresses."

"They will open a stand especially for dresses and dress suits on Wednesday for the occasion. Maybe we can shop together and try dresses on?"

"Sure." I said. I didn't want to disappoint her by turning her down. Besides, her kindness and interest were starting to grow on me.

She whispered to me, "Did you find a date yet?"

"No. And don't want one."

"Oh, come on! You have to have a date!"

"Says who?"

"Well, everybody goes with a date."

"Who are you going with?" I asked

"I don't know yet. You know who I would like to go with, but it will never happen," she said.

CHAPTER FIFTEEN

Miss Grace, Miss Pomegrade, Mr. Corrigan, and I met again at 9 p.m.

"I used the serum this morning and found a portal to teleport people across the forbidden place, and—"

"You what?" asked Miss Grace.

"Ashley, you shouldn't have gone alone. You don't know how dangerous that could have been," said Collin.

"Anyway, I think I discovered where they hide their supplies. We should spy there first," I said.

"You never cease to amaze me," said Miss Pomegrade.

"Oh, I also saw a man bleeding to death. His arm was cut off and another whose face was burnt…and people with guns…and I heard a weird loud …animal noise?"

"That's insane! It's not like we're at war. It must be some sort of danger zone," said Miss Pomegrade.

"I think so, or maybe they are experimenting with their serum on animals? Whatever it was, it sure wasn't a pretty sight." I replied.

We each drank a cup of serum, waited to become invisible, and walked in the direction of the portal. It was very dark outside and hard to see where we were going. A flashlight would've given us away, so we relied on our night vision. When we stepped on the sticks I made an X with, I knew we'd reached the portal. We teleported across the forbidden place.

"The building is in this hill," I said, pointing at where I'd seen the door open.

"You're kidding, right?" said Collin.

"No. We can't see it from here, but there's a door. Let's go. I'm sure if we get closer, we'll see it," I said.

If it weren't for the doorknob, we wouldn't have found the door. Even from close up, the door was still hidden. We looked around us to see if anybody was there, but we were all alone. Everything was silent.

"You would think someone would be guarding the door if this was it," Collin said.

As he put his hand on the doorknob, the door opened and hit Collin in the face. Collin took a few steps back, holding his forehead and biting his tongue to not scream in pain. A man came out, looking confused.

"Well, that's funny, I could have sworn the door hit something," said the man to the man behind him.

We were all standing a few inches away, waiting to go in. I went to see if Collin was OK. I put my left hand on his arm and my right one on his forehead. Miss Grace gave me a grin, but I ignored her. I asked him telepathically if he was OK. He nodded, then he added, "Watch it. Miss Grace is looking at us." I took my hand off but stayed beside him.

"Well, there's nothing around. Maybe you hit a bug or something."

"No, it was something bigger. I even heard a bump."

"Are you going to just stand there all night, or are we going for a smoke?"

"I know I hit something, man."

"Maybe the serum is affecting you."

"I didn't even touch the serum."

"Well, maybe it's the stress and working overtime. Come on, man, we only have five minutes."

As soon as the second man came outside, we quickly went in. The door led us to a tunnel that we followed until it sectioned off into three separate tunnels. We didn't know where to go. We had to choose between Gate 1, Gate 2, and Gate 3 or turning around, but we didn't know which one to take.

"Let's split. Ashley, come with me in Gate 1. Grace, take Gate 2, and Miss Pomegrade, take Gate 3. Let's take just a quick peek and come back here in fifteen minutes. The clock is ticking."

We went our separate ways, sprinting down the tunnels, but stopped when we saw two men coming from around the corner. They were both wearing white togas, white gloves, and masks.

"Did you hear that?" asked one of the men.

"Hear what?" said the other.

"Sounded like footsteps," said the first man.

"It couldn't have been."

"Shit!" said the first man.

"What?"

"I forgot my cellphone."

"Geez. Let's go back then. But hurry, it's been a long day," said the other man.

"You go right ahead. I'll catch up to you," said the first man.

"You know the rules—never cross alone."

"That's horseshit!"

"Hey, I didn't make the rules."

They both turned around and walked back to wherever they had come from. We followed them closely. They came to a sealed door with a security code, so I looked over one of the men's shoulder to see his code. He punched in 2234. The door unlocked and opened on its own. I waved Collin to follow, and we walked in right behind them. The lab we walked into was huge. A few men were making a serum; two women were carefully measuring the flask and labelling it. A young man was transporting a flask to a reservoir, so we decided to follow him. He punched in his security code: 2252. Inside was a huge storage room with shelving units everywhere that read SERUM OF DESTRUCTION and LETHAL SERUM. There it was, right before our eyes! Collin looked at his watch. He said to me, "Time to go!" We snuck out with the young man. When nobody was paying attention to the exit door, we got out and sprinted back to the four-way intersection. Miss Grace and Miss Pomegrade were already there. "You're late!" said an unhappy Miss Grace.

We only had fifteen minutes left, so we had to get back to the portal as soon as possible. There was no time to talk. At the exit door, there was no way to tell if someone was behind the door or not, but we couldn't afford to wait. Again, when Collin put his hand on the handle, the door opened.

He almost fell forward this time. Three men came inside. Seth was one of them, so was Martin Pump. Miss Grace's face dropped when she saw him, but we had no choice but to get out. Collin pulled her out of the building before the door closed on her. We sprinted back to the portal and crossed the forbidden place. As soon as we were in the safe zone, we teleported back to Collin's school.

"That was a close call. What took you two so long?" asked Miss Grace.

"We found the serum supply, and it's huge," said Collin.

"No way!"

"What about you guys?" I asked.

"I found the surveillance room. There are on twenty-four/seven. The bathrooms, the schools, and the dormitories are about the only places that are not covered. Eight people were watching the live feeds," said Miss Grace.

"Unreal!" said Collin.

"What about you, Miss Pomegrade?" I asked.

"There were three jet airplanes. They were trying to hook an infuser on… for the serum of destruction, I presume."

Just then I felt my serum fading, and shortly after, all the others were visible as well.

"Now we know what we're up against. But the question is, how we can destroy it?" asked Collin.

"Good question," I said.

"It's very late. How about we sleep on it? I myself found it very nerve-wracking and exhausting," said Miss Pomegrade.

"Fair enough. Let's meet back here same time, same place tomorrow with a rested mind," said Collin.

Miss Pomegrade teleported back home, followed by Miss Grace. I was about to leave, when Collin said, "Not so fast, missy."

I looked at him with a questioning look. He got closer and stared into my eyes.

"Did you forget something?"

"No. I don't think so?"

"This." He leaned down and kissed me. "I've been craving one of those all night."

I couldn't help but smile. I wondered what he felt about me. His mind didn't show any malice, but it hit me that although I could read people's minds, I couldn't read their hearts. It never struck me as important to know how people felt inside. I always thought reading minds was the same, but it wasn't. It was easy to read people's mind—or at least it was for me—but what did I know about people's feeling? Nothing. I'd never been in love, never had a true friend, except for Antoinette. I didn't know what love was. Right this moment, I wished I could read his feelings because when I was near him, my heart was racing and I couldn't stop thinking of him night and day, wishing I could be alone with him. Maybe this was love? It reminded me of my brother and Antoinette. Now I was starting to get why they were so inseparable. The thought of my brother and Antoinette made me nostalgic. I wondered how he was coping with life now that his love was gone. I wondered how my family was. It had been a lifetime since I had seen them, since I had talked to them. Right this moment, I longed to see them, to introduce Collin to them. I was sure

Collin and my brother would get along. I wondered what they thought happened to me. They must have been worried. I made a mental note to try to somehow make contact with them, to let them know I was OK.

"What's wrong, Ash?"

"Nothing."

"Come on, Ash. Something is obviously bothering you."

"I was just thinking of my family for some reason. Does your family know you are here?"

"No."

"When was the last time you talked to them?"

"Mmm, a good two years. Why?"

"I just think it's cruel to leave them in the dark like this. They should at least know we are OK."

"And tell them what? That we are trapped on a wizard island forever, that they are trying to destroy the world, and that we are stupidly trying to save it? What good would that do?"

"At least they would know that I am alive."

"The thing is, there is no way to communicate with them from here. If we could somehow get off this island, things would be different. But right now, for a wizard who was not born here, friends are the closest thing to a family...and right now, I feel so close to you, I can't explain it. It's like you are my family. You are the only person who I feel close to on this island and the only person I want to spend time with. It's like we were meant to be together. Wow, I can't believe this. I sound like such a sap."

"I know what you mean. I feel the same way about you. And I feel like I have known you my entire life. Who knows, maybe we shared past lives together."

"That's possible. Hey, that gives me an idea. Are you tired?"

"I couldn't sleep even if I wanted to. Why?"

"Do you trust me?" he asked.

"I don't know. Should I?"

"Come with me."

We teleported to the Healing School.

"What are we doing here?"

"How about we do some time traveling together, see if we shared lives together."

"Sounds good, but we won't remember once we are awake."

"I have the cure for that." He showed me a DVD. "We will record our session."

"Can we do that?"

"I don't know. Can't hurt to try though."

"Have you done this with someone else before?"

"Are you kidding me? No. Not in a million years would I reveal my past to someone. Set yourself up and drink half the serum. Leave the rest for me. The effect should last for at least twenty minutes. I'll press record and be right there. Save me a place with you. We are going to share the same chair."

I knew the drill well enough now, and so did Collin. It didn't take him long to join me. I laid my head on his chest with both of our hands joined together. It didn't take long before we traveled to the past.

Collin and I were brother and sister. Collin was older and was very protective of me. We were running away from our dad in the bush. In the middle of the night, our parents had had a big fight. Like usual, Dad had come home drunk and was in a bad mood. He had played poker and lost all of his money. Our mom said something about it, and our dad lost it. He started beating our mother, and when he was finished, we weren't sure if she was dead, but she looked dead. Dad was still throwing things in the kitchen. Collin decided that it was best to run away. He had helped me escape though my bedroom window, and we ran as fast as we could. We didn't know where we were going, but we kept running. After a few minutes, we heard our dad scream our names at the top of his lungs: "Julie! Dawson!" Dawson had put his hand on my mouth to make sure I wouldn't answer his call.

I knew what we had to do. We had to confront our dad. Running away was not the answer. We needed to face the problem. Together we walked back to our dad. He was a mess. At first, he was very mad that we had run away, but when our dad realized what he had done, he fell on his knees and started to cry. He begged us for forgiveness, and when we granted him forgiveness, the scene cleared away. We had just cleared another life.

We were young lovers and very happy at the time. We were walking on train tracks when we saw a train coming from afar. Collin jumped off the tracks. I stayed on them. I wanted to see how close I could get to the train before I chickened out and jumped off.

"Patricia, come on! That's not funny!"

"Don't be such a chicken shit, Blaze!"

"Geez, Pat, jump off! Have you lost your mind?"

I just laughed and continued to watch the train as it came closer and closer. It was getting so close that my whole body was shaking from the vibrations on the tracks. Blaze was screaming something at me, but I couldn't hear anything. Finally, he jumped on the track and pushed me off, but he got hit by the train and I survived.

"No!" I screamed. But it was too late. He was dead. He had died saving my life. I felt so ashamed and guilty, I wanted to die.

I knew what I had to do. I felt so terrible. I truly loved him. My soul found his, and I begged for forgiveness. I told him that I had been very stupid and I didn't mean for him to die. That, in fact, I was very much in love with him and I would rather die than lose him. Blaze didn't let me finish. He gave me a hug and forgave me. We cleared another life together.

When the effect of the serum had faded away, I woke up in Collin's arms. We were both sweaty. We couldn't remember what happened. We went to look at the recording. We were amazed to see our past lives together. It confirmed the fact that we had spent two of our lives together, and we were sure there were many more. But it was very late, and we both had school the next day, so we agreed to keep this a secret, erased the recording, and called it a day.

CHAPTER SIXTEEN

Veronica, Stephany, and I spent hours trying on dresses, but I couldn't find one that was my type. I didn't want anything too fancy. I didn't care about the dance or impressing anybody...except Collin, of course. I didn't know if the teachers had to be there, but sadly, I didn't have a choice in the matter. I had to go, according to Veronica. Both Veronica and Stephany had found the perfect match within the first half hour. After an hour, I still didn't have a dress.

"What about this one?" asked Veronica.

"Not for me."

"Oh, come on, Ashley! Just pick one! I'm hungry, and it's time for supper," said Stephany.

"Go, you two. I'll meet you back at the table shortly."

Veronica hesitated before saying, "Are you sure?"

"Yes, I'm sure. Go!"

Once I was alone, I was able to listen to my heart and let it pick one suitable for me. My heart chose a bright light blue one. It was simple yet elegant. It went two inches above my knees and made a V down my back.

I tried it on, and it fit me perfectly. All I had to do was give my name to the seller; the seller crossed my name off the list before I left. I teleported to my room, put the dress away, and went to the cafeteria. I was happy to see Collin there, but it was hard to pretend that nothing was going on between us...he was on my mind twenty-four/seven. I knew he was a distraction to my mission. The timing was not the greatest to fall in love; unfortunately, it was not something I had control over.

After supper, I went to train at the Warriors School. The last time I had been there was the time Steven and his friends attacked me. I was reluctant to go, afraid of seeing him there. It really was the last place I wanted to be alone right now, but the tournament was in two days, and I wanted to be ready for it. That was all the students were talking about at the tables. Even the teachers were talking about it.

For once, the school was packed with students. Apparently, I was not the only one getting ready for the tournament. The students present were mostly from the Warriors devotion, including Steven. I pretended I wasn't intimidated by him, even though I was. I figured because it was so packed, Steven couldn't hurt me in front of everybody, so I felt somewhat safe.

My shooting skills were getting better, but I definitely wasn't the best, not by a long shot. My theory was that it was because shooting was a solitary skill, and therefore I didn't have the advantage of reading the target's mind, like I did when fighting an opponent. I was sure it would be different if the target I was shooting at was a human, but I hoped it would never come to that.

I trained until 8 p.m., and then I went to my room and took a long shower. I wanted to look good for Collin. My mind was racing, like it had been all day, trying to figure out a perfect plan to destroy the serum of destruction.

I teleported to the Warriors School at 9:01 p.m. I was the last one to arrive.

"I'm sorry I took my time. Did I keep you waiting?" I asked.

"No, we just got here too," said Miss Grace.

"Anybody found a solution to our impossible mission?" asked Collin.

"I say we blow up the warehouse at night time. That would for sure destroy it," proposed Miss Grace.

"Absolutely not! The heat would evaporate the serum, causing the activation of the serum and diffusing it into the air, killing anybody who would breathe," I replied.

"Well, what do you suggest, Einstein?" said Miss Grace.

"How about we steal the serum and drop it in the sea?" proposed Miss Pomegrade.

"And how are we supposed to steal the whole warehouse without being seen? And how are we going to drop it in the sea when it's off limits?" asked Collin.

"I didn't think of all the details..."

"Have you two come up with a better plan, or are you just going to judge ours?" asked Miss Grace.

"Who said we were judging?" replied Collin.

"If we want to destroy the serum, we have to create some sort of an antidote to neutralize the liquid. We would need to go back in the warehouse, and we would have to dump all the serum of destruction in one big cauldron to neutralize it. Same with the lethal serum and the back-up in the president's safe. To succeed, we would have to kidnap all the employees and erase their memories. One of us would have to watch over the kidnaped employees, while the other three would work on the antidote. I know it's a long shot, but that's all I could think of," I said.

"I love your devotion, but how are we supposed to create an antidote?" asked Collin.

"That's the easy part. I already know what we need. We need to use the antidotes for each poisonous ingredient. All I need to do is test it on one of the flasks to see if it works before we risk this operation."

"What are the ingredients?" asked Miss Pomegrade.

I took a piece of paper from my pockets and gave it to her.

"Of course! You are a genius! And I have just about every ingredient...but we need to find out the amounts needed."

"I know. That means someone would have to duplicate into a tarantula and bite one of us. Then I would have to try a calculated dose of the antidote needed for the venom in the person. That will determine the proportion needed per flask."

"Count me out. I have a phobia of spiders, never mind tarantulas," said Miss Grace.

"I would do it, but I need to create and calculate the antidote, and I can't do that if I duplicated into a tarantula," I said.

"OK, I will do it. I will duplicate into a tarantula," said Miss Pomegrade.

"Then I will be the brave victim," said Collin.

"I'll be your doctor," I said, giving him a wink.

"Are you guys really serious about this?" asked Miss Grace.

"Of course we are. Let's do this," said Collin, clapping his hands.

"First, I need to work in the Grounding School to create the antidote for the tarantula venom, the scorpion venom, and the rattlesnake venom. The dosage should be the same. In the meantime, maybe you two could drink the invisible serum and go steal a flask while I work with Miss Pomegrade to save time," I said.

"Now that I can do, but don't count on me being here with the tarantula," said Miss Grace.

"Please be careful, and hurry back to the Grounding School," I begged.

"Should be a walk in a park. I know the way and the security code," reassured Collin.

Miss Grace and Collin were off to the warehouse while Miss Pomegrade and I teleported to the Grounding School. Within twenty-five minutes, I had created the antidotes for the venoms and assembled all the ingredients for the destruction serum antidote. Miss Pomegrade helped me find all the ingredients I needed. Then we worked on the antidote for the lethal serum. This one was easier; it took us only ten minutes. We just had to add the right amount of the venom's antidotes to the serum and we could complete our mission. I asked Miss Pomegrade if she knew the quantity of venom per bite.

"About one-quarter teaspoon of venom. It's not much, but it's fatal."

Shortly after, Miss Grace and Collin arrived with two flasks, one of the destruction serum and the other with the lethal serum. They looked proud of themselves.

"Well done. Now let's get started. Miss Pomegrade, drink this duplicate serum, and don't forget to visualize a tarantula while you drink it," I ordered.

"See ya! I'm out of here. I'll wait in the locker room. Good luck!" said Miss Grace.

Miss Pomegrade seemed to be in pain for a moment, and then one arm at a time became a spider leg, then her legs. Then her torso became a thorax. For a couple of seconds, she looked half human, half tarantula, with her face still human. When Miss Pomegrade became a complete tarantula, Collin took the spider in his hand and placed it on his arm. It bit him. Collin tried not to scream and pushed the spider off his arm. Miss Pomegrade hid in a corner, profusely apologizing in her thoughts.

Collin's arm was already getting swollen and red. I immediately took his arm and injected precisely one-quarter teaspoon of the serum. The effect was instant: The redness disappeared; so did the inflammation.

"Just what I thought. We need the same amount of antidote for the venom to be neutralized. How do you feel?" I asked.

"Good. Better now, actually. The pain is completely gone. Good job, Ash! You did it!"

When Miss Pomegrade became herself again, we called Miss Grace in. We prepared and placed all the ingredients we'd need in backpacks and agreed we would attack the next day at 10 p.m. The first day of the tournament would be a good distraction to all the people on the island. We would wait for the fireworks to start. Nobody would pay attention to our whereabouts then. We decided that Collin would evacuate the building by infusing the manipulation serum into the building's air, hide all the staff in the bush nearby, and then guard them while the rest of us would go to the warehouse. We would go back to Mr. Blake's office another day to destroy the backup.

CHAPTER SEVENTEEN

The ambiance was hypnotizing. Hundreds of witches and wizards of all ages were gathered in the stadium. The fabulios ball field was about the size of a football field. The five devotion house players were distinguish by their respective jerseys, each wearing their own colors: The Grounding School in green, the Healing School in violet, the Warriors School in black, the Teleportation School in red, and the Formula School in gold. The first game started at 9 a.m., the Teleportation School vs. the Grounding School. Not surprising, the Teleportation School was leading 3-0 after only twenty minutes into the game. It was very exciting. I watched how the game was played. The principle was easy enough to follow. All you had to do was teleport the ball into your opponent's ring, trying to escape from the obstacle to avoid any deviation to the ball. Only, you had to have superb teleportation skills to be able to move and control the ball with speed. As expected, the Teleportation School players were masters at the game. The Grounding School players had trouble teleporting the ball and controlling it. It was bouncing on the walls everywhere. By the end of the hour, the Teleportation School won 12-0; the Grounding School was eliminated. We were playing the next game against the Warriors School. Only eight players were allowed on the field. I started the game on the bench, Mr. Hunter's orders. He had said that because I had never played the game before, I would be useless on the field. He wanted to win this game. He desperately wanted to get to the finals this year.

After fifteen minutes, we were behind 2-0. We didn't have enough strong players to win. Veronica dared talk to Mr. Hunter, saying she should be the one benched because she couldn't teleport yet and I was the best one in the class. He hated to put me on the field, but he had no choice if he wanted to win. As soon as I went on the field, I took control of the ball and within ten seconds scored our first goal. The game was easy; all I had to do was listen to the players' mind, and I knew what they were going to do before they'd done it. I also had to keep my eyes on every corner to follow the movement of the walls and elevation of the floor. I was always one step ahead of my opponents. Steven was an aggressive player and obviously didn't like to lose. When we were leading 5-2 after forty minutes, he teleported my way and knocked me down, hitting my right kneecap. He made it look like an accident, but I knew it was intentional. My leg was injured, I was limping, but the game went on. Collin tried not to look worried, but he couldn't fool me. When Steven knocked me down, I heard Mr. Hunter scream, "Oh, come on! Penalty shoot! He did it on purpose! He injured my best player!"

Mr. Hunter had no choice but to put me on the bench. I could barely walk. He gave me ice to put on my knee. The game went on. I started to heal myself privately; nobody paid attention to me. With five minutes left in the game, we were losing 6-5.

"Mr. Hunter, my knee feels better now. I'm ready to go back on the field."

"You can't be. Your knee looked dislocated."

"It obviously wasn't. Look. The ice did the trick." Another score from the Warriors team had the crowd roaring. It was 7-5 now.

"Fine."

Mr. Hunter called time out and put Veronica on the bench and me on the field. The Warriors players were waiting for me this time, and they all came at me at once, blocking me. That didn't stop me from teleporting to the other side of the field where they didn't expect me to go. Before they knew it, I had taken control of the ball and scored. It was 7-6. Steven was ballistic. He started screaming at his teammates, blaming them for letting me have the ball, so I decided to have a little fun with him. I took control of the ball, made it hit Steven's forehead, and when it bounced, I scored, tying the game. The crowd roared louder this time. I heard Steven's mind say, "You're gonna pay for this." I just smiled at him. There were thirty seconds left in the game. Steven had control of the ball and was going toward our ring. I took control of the ball too but didn't let it show it. When he went to score, I made the ball hit the ring and bounced it on his forehead again. This time he fell onto his back. The crowd was laughing and cheering. I scored within five seconds of the end of the game, and we won 8-7. Amazingly, we eliminated the Warriors School. All of my teammates came running at me and lifted me up in the air. Steven was still on the ground. He was OK; he was just faking being knocked out to avoid the embarrassment of losing against the Formula School.

The Teleportation School dominated the third game against the Healing School. The Healing School had good players, but they stood no chance against the Teleportation School, and in the end, the Teleportation School won 8-2. Then it was lunchtime; we had forty-five minutes to eat before the finals began. There was a BBQ near the ring, and all the players were served before the crowd. When Collin passed beside me, he told me telepathically, "Hey, turn it down a notch, will you? People are noticing your unusual skills. The last thing you want is to be noticed today."

I knew he was just giving me friendly advice, but he almost sounded mad or jealous. Was he mad at me because they lost? His mind was telling me that yes, indeed he was.

"I can't believe how good you are at that game!" said Mel.

"Never mind good. She is amazing!" said Veronica.

"Are you sure you've never played it before?" asked Mel.

"Oh, come on! You're just jealous!" teased Julius.

"Yes, I am sure. It's an easy game."

"Not that easy. Makes me wonder..." said Stephany.

"Wonder what?" I asked.

"How did you do it? Maybe you have some superpowers that we don't have, and you just refuse to admit it."

I was about to reply when a bunch of people came toward me and gave me high fives; some even wanted my autograph. I didn't know how to react to this. Maybe Collin was right after all; maybe I was attracting too much attention. I decided to keep a low profile for the finals.

"It was just beginner's luck" was my answer to both Stephany and my fans.

Nobody looked convinced. For the finals, the Teleportation School players were much stronger. It was a good game. I kept the score close the whole game but let them win by one point in the end. My plan had been to play well enough to make my team and Mr. Hunter think I had done my best, but the glory would go to the Teleportation School as usual. My plan worked. Everybody was cheering for the Teleportation School instead of me. Everyone forgot about me after this game—well, almost everyone. Steven didn't forget about me; no, he wanted me dead, he wanted sweet revenge.

When I walked by Collin, he told me telepathically, "Well done!"

On the scoreboard, written in big letters were the points we'd earned.

Teleportation School: 3 points
Formula School: 2 points
Warriors School: 0 points
Healing School: 0 points
Grounding School: 0 points

My team and Mr. Hunter seemed pleased with that result. In the middle of the ring, the staff installed five tables. Cameras were fixed on the tables and projected to big screens. It was the Formulas Event. Mr. Hunter used his ring as a microphone and said, "Ladies and gentlemen, the Formula School's challenge for this year's tournament is to create a serum that will make an object disappear when you put a drop on it. On the shelf, you will find everything you need and more for this serum. You can only rely on your common sense. You don't have access to your formula volume. You will have precisely one hour to create the serum of disappearance. It's teamwork. The first team to succeed will win. If by the end of the hour no team has succeeded, all the teams will receive a zero for that challenge. Good luck!"

"OMG, we will never make it! How in the hell can we come up with a serum like that?" said Mel.

"Last year's was easier: the sleepless serum. We won first place and were up all night, thanks to the serum. But this year, wow! I'm clueless!" said Julius.

"OK, let's put our brains together and think. There's got to be a way," said Veronica.

All the team members were still whispering to each other. Nobody got up and grabbed ingredients. I think they were all waiting for the first group to lead, and normally that would be the Formula School.

"Do you trust me, guys?" I asked them.

"Yes, why?" asked Veronica.

I grabbed a piece of paper and a pencil, and I said, "This is what we need. All of us will have to discretely measure half a cup of one of the ingredients and hide it under our shirt so no other team sees what we take."

> Daucus Carota essence
> Beauty flower essence
> Javex
> Peroxide
> Chlorine

"Are you sure about this?" asked Stephany.

"95 percent sure."

I assigned each an ingredient, paired in twos. When we got up and started getting the ingredients, the others teams got up too to snoop around. When we hid them under our shirts, they looked even more puzzled. Nobody was allowed at our table, so it was safe to work once we were back. I took charge of the mixing. My mind and my heart were telling me what to do. Once I was done, I said, "OK. This is it."

"Are you sure?" asked Veronica.

"Look, do you have another solution or idea?"

"No."

"Thought so."

Julius rang the bell. Mr. Hunter came along and spoke into his ring again.

"The first attempt is done by the Formula School. This is kind of premature...it only took you twenty minutes. But you rang the bell, and rules are rules. Who wants to do the honors and place a drop on the book I am holding?"

All eyes looked to me. I put the gloves on, took the flask on the table, and dipped it in the serum. I held the full flask and tilted it over the book. One drop fell. Everybody at my table held their breaths and crossed their fingers. When the book became invisible, my teammates jumped with excitement and hugged me. The crowd went wild.

"Ladies and gentlemen, we have a winner! This point goes to the Formula School," Mr. Hunter said, trying to hide his excitement.

"How did you know?" asked Stephany.

"I trusted and listened to my gut feeling, that's all," I replied.

"Well, thank God for your gut feeling!" said Mel.

"Amen!" added Julius.

The teachers cleared the materials and tables to get ready for the next event. I was laughing with my teammates when Collin approached our table. He looked upset, and our eyes met. He told me telepathically, "You call that low profile?" He had done it again—ruined my mood, my glory. I looked at him but didn't say anything. What was there to say? What did he expect me to do? Play dumb and lose? I would like to see what he would have done in my place. Why did he have to be so serious all the time?

* * * * *

The middle of the ring was set up like a clinic: separate rooms, one for each devotion house, with a bed and medical kit. It reminded me of my aptitude test at the Ascendant School. The idea was the same. We had to play doctor and find a cure for a disease. Dressed like a doctor, Miss Pomegrade escorted in the ill patient. I was shocked to see the simulation: here was Collin, weak, white as a ghost, in a wheelchair. My heart sank to see him like this. I was tempted to run to him, but I had to remind myself that this was just a simulation.

"Good afternoon, doctors. I have with me Mr. Corrigan. He was brought here this morning from emergency by ambulance." She showed his arms and legs. Everybody gasped; I put my two hands over my mouth. "He was diagnosed with *Morgellons*, a chronic bacterial disease. Sadly, the disease usually is disfiguring as well as disabling. The disease is classified by biting, itching, or crawling sensations, filaments that grow from the skin, and skin lesions, as well as memory loss, joint paint, and fatigue. You have an hour to find a cure to save Mr. Corrigan. You may use any of the natural ingredients on the shelves. It's an uncommon disease and there-fore should be treated with caution. Of course, books are not permitted for this event. Good luck!"

Collin was writhing in pain, and it killed me to see him suffer like this. I was determinate to find a cure, even if it meant not keeping a low profile.

"OK, I think I know what we need," I said.

"Surprise, surprise," said Stephany.

"This is what we need: aloe leaves, vitamin E, raw honey, activated char-coal, and a few drops of tea tree oil."

"OK, I can see why the aloe leaves and vitamin E. That's pretty common. But why honey and charcoal, and…"

"Activated charcoal draws out toxins extremely well and can eliminate harmful bacteria as well. The raw honey is to make the charcoal into a paste; otherwise, it would make a powdery mess, and besides, honey has antibacterial qualities and is known to help heal other types of infec-tions. The tea tree essential oil has antiseptic and antiviral qualities," I replied impatiently.

"OK, I trust you. Let's do this," said Mel.

"What measurements do we need?" asked Veronica.

"Let's start with a cup of activated charcoal and a cup of honey, a full aloe leaf, half a cup of the vitamin E, and half a cup of the tea tree oil," I suggested.

"Do we still have to hide our ingredients?" asked Julius.

"I think it would be wise to," I replied.

We went to get our ingredients, hiding them again in our shirts. I made the mixture; it was black, thick, a bit goopy, and gross looking.

"Ta-da!" I said when I was finish. My heart was confident it would work.

Julius rang the bell. Miss Pomegrade came running to our table. She looked surprised that her own devotion house had not come up with anything yet.

"Well, well! The Formula School is full of surprises today. Who would like to spread that cream on your poor teacher?"

Again, all eyes went to me. I got up and walked toward Collin, looking into his eyes. He looked at me with despair. He was in so much pain. I applied the cream first on his arms, then on his legs. He screamed and flinched. His hives were sizzling, and yellow pus came out of them. The cameras had zoomed in to see the effect of the healing cream attempt. I hated to see him suffer like this; gladly, his pain soon turned to relief. The red spots got smaller and smaller, lighter and lighter, until they completely disappeared. I could hear the crowd cheering and applauding.

"Thank you!" said Collin.

"You are welcome, Mr. Corrigan."

"Incredible! We have a winner! One point for the Formula School!" said Miss Pomegrade.

My team went ballistic. We were now leading the tournament. The Grounding School students were protesting, saying we cheated.

"All right, all right, calm down students. Sometimes you win, sometimes you lose. It's part of life. Nobody cheated," said Miss Pomegrade.

They were now setting up a big fighting ring in the middle of the tournament field. This time Mr. Corrigan took the stand and talked into his ring.

"Ladies and gentlemen, it's time for the kickboxing tournament. Each devotion house will fight each other for twenty minutes. Any member is allowed to rotate turns by tapping out if need be. The team players have to determine the order of the fighters thirty seconds before the fight starts. At the end of the twenty minutes, the fight will stop, and the judges will determine the winner. The judges are the five teachers and Master Thunderstone. The losers will be eliminated; the winners will continue on in the fighting competition. Master Thunderstone will have the honor of picking the two first teams. Good luck to you all."

The elimination process went fairly fast. After one hour of intense fighting, two teams were left: the Warriors School against the Formula School for the finals.

During the thirty-second discussion, I tried to listen to the minds of my opponents. They were going to start with their two fastest to ward off our best. Joshua was the third, and Steven was the fourth.

"Listen. How about we start with Stephany? She's very fast."

"But I'm not a good fighter."

"But they won't expect us to start with you. They expect us to start with the best, so we should do the opposite. Besides, you can tap out when you want to. You don't have to wait until you are injured."

"I think that's a great idea," said Julius.

"Veronica, you go second, Julius, go third, Mel, fourth, and I'll be the fifth. The rest of you have ten seconds to decide."

The bell rang. Stephany jumped in as well as her opponent, a fast and agile girl. It was funny to see the surprised faces from the Warriors team. They'd not seen that one coming. They had expected Mel to come in. Steven was right; the girl was very fast, but so was Stephany. They danced for the first three minutes without any actions. It was boring to watch, and the crowd was booing, so they both decided to tap out.

Veronica went in, and so did another girl. Veronica's opponent was twice her size. One punch in the ribs and Veronica tapped out. Julius went in, monkeylike, and tripped the girl. She didn't even try to come back, and she tapped out. Joshua came in.

Julius tried to trip him many times but failed. Joshua had skills and knocked Julius out with one jab to the face. He tapped out and Mel went in. It was a much better match. They fought for the next five minutes, punching back and forth, both still standing. Joshua jabbed him in the jaw. Mel tapped out.

Before I got in, I said to Veronica, "Now don't be mad. I have no choice if we want to win." She nodded. I jumped in. We dance for the first two minutes. I managed to avoid all of his hits. He was getting tired. He wasn't expecting a kick in the ribs. He was out of breath. I jabbed him in the jaw, and he fell down. I could hear Steven scream, "Tap out! That bitch is mine!" and he did. Steven jumped in quickly and tried to hit me like a mad man. One on one, I was able to read his mind, prevent and avoid his moves. The more he missed, the madder he got. I punched him hard in the face and caught him by surprise. He was bleeding but still standing strong, so I punched him again on the other side of his temple and then kicked him in the ribs. This fight was personal; it was payback time. For the first time, I truly wanted to hurt my opponent. There was blood in the ring—Steven's blood. His left eye was swollen, and the crowd was wild. He could barely stand, but Steven was too proud to tap out. I had him cornered. I could finish him. I was about to punch him when I heard Collin screaming at me telepathically, "Low profile, Ash! You can't win against him. He is the best!" I gave him a look of disbelief. The few seconds that Collin distracted me were the saving grace for Steven. He punched me in the face and broke my nose. I was knocked down.

Now it was my turn to bleed. I wanted to punch him so badly but decided to tap out instead, at Collin's request. A tall, quiet boy who I didn't know very well jumped in next. Steven knocked him down on the first punch. A girl jumped in, already crying because she was facing him. He kicked her in the stomach. She fell down, and as she fell down, the bell rang. Mr. Corrigan announced the winner shortly after. "The winner and unde-feated team is the Warriors School! The Formula School is out!" he said in an all too happy, proud tone. I was disgusted by him right now. I could have finished Steven if it hadn't been for Collin. When he looked at me, I turned my back on him. My nose and my head were killing me. I couldn't heal myself right this moment, not when everybody knew I had a broken nose. I had to endure the pain. I was shocked when Mr. Hunter came to me and said, "Here, drink this serum. It will stop the bleeding." I didn't know if I should trust him. His mind was telling me that he was telling the truth, so I drank it. The bleeding stopped. "Thanks" was all I managed to say.

There was a forty-five-minute pause for dinner. This time, it was steaks and potatoes on the BBQ. I was starving; we all were. There was a variety of different salads. When I was serving myself with my raccoon eyes, Collin came and served himself too. "Ash, listen to me..." he started.

"Leave me alone," I replied. And on that, I turned my back and went to sit with my teammates. Nobody was talking at the table. Everybody was devouring their dinner. When we started dessert, Julius said, "I thought for sure you had Steven, that that was the end of him. What happened?"

"I thought so too, but in the end, he got me and won. Can we change subject please?"

"I'm not blaming you. Don't get me wrong."

"Just drop it, OK?"

"Fine."

"Oh, you two, stop with the long faces. We are still leading the tournament," said Veronica.

"Ready for the next challenge?" asked Stephany.

"Yes, why?"

"Because I'm sure they are going to pick you."

"Now why is that?"

"Like you don't know."

"Actually, no, I don't."

"They always pick the best one of each devotion house. We can't all participate—it would take too long—so they pick the highest scoring students, and they simulate one of your pasts that they recorded…and they manipulate the facts," explained Mel.

"I really hope it's not me," I replied.

"Why? Because you have some deep, dark secrets?" said Stephany.

"Now why do you have to be like that?" said Julius.

* * * * *

Everybody was back at the ring when Miss Grace took the stand and talked to her ring, "Good evening, ladies and gentlemen. Welcome to the last challenge of the day. As usual, we have taken the highest scoring student from each devotion house for this last event. The chosen student will have to face a manipulated simulation of their past that was the most challenging to clear. They will need to deal with it and clear the past memory. Because it is a simulation of a past already cleared, you will remember the simulation when you wake up. Each simulation will be timed. The images will be posted on the big screen, live. The student who manages to clear his or her past the fastest will win this challenge. In this bucket, we have four names. Master Thunderstone will have the honor of picking the first chosen. Good luck to you all."

"Good evening, wizards and witches. The first chosen is Ashley Connors from the Formula School."

The crowd cheered for me as I walked to the center of the ring, sat in the chair, and drank the pink serum. It didn't take me long to fall back in time to an all too familiar place.

Steven was leading the way with Brittany on his back. Brandon and I shared the second quad, Justin and Antoinette were behind us, and Cole and Alex were the last ones. We had already been gone for a couple of hours. We were all covered in mud. I couldn't remember the last time I had laughed so much. I was holding on tight to Brandon. He didn't seem to mind it. In fact, he seemed to like it. When I let go of him, he would grab my hands softly, put them on his hips, and say, "Hang on!"

We came to a sand pit. There were quads everywhere. People were driving crazy, doing jumps and all. Steven and Brittany decided to play in the sand pit for a while, and the rest of us decided to continue on because we were hungry.

"Stay on the main trail; it will bring you straight to the trailer park. I'll catch up to you. I just want to try a couple of jumps," Steven said to his younger brother, Brandon.

"OK. Be careful," replied Brandon.

Brandon was now leading. We were cruising along, enjoying the perfect weather for the perfect ride on a perfect day. On the side of the trail, we saw two does. Brandon pointed them out to me. They ran away gracefully. Brandon pretended to accidently put his hand on mine. When he saw that I didn't take it away, he squeezed it gently. It felt good and made me feel funny from the inside. It was the first time in my life that a boy had held my hand willingly. My heart was beating fast. In front of us was a big curve. We slowed down.

We noticed that nobody was behind us. Brandon stopped the quad, and we waited for them to catch up to us. He turned around and took off his helmet. I took off mine too. We looked into each other's eyes, then he leaned down. His face was so close to mine. He gently kissed me. I kissed him back.

We heard a loud, awful scream. We quickly put our helmets back on, turned the quad around, and went toward the scream. Not even a mile away we saw quads in the middle of the trail. We stopped dead when we saw what was going on. Brittany was crying in Steven arms, and Alex was sitting in the ditch, white as a ghost. Cole was screaming and crying in despair. There'd obviously been an accident. Brandon took out his cellphone and called 911.

I didn't see her at first. I concentrated on what Brandon was saying. They were sending a Star helicopter and two ambulances right away. I didn't quite understand the extent of the accident. I was too absorbed by the others' reactions. Why were they crying? Why were they wondering if she was dead? Who were they talking about? And then I saw the reason for the panic.

Immobile, lying in a weird position was a girl covered in blood. Her left eye seemed to be missing. It was so swollen. Blood had come out of her mouth; her neck was placed in an unnatural angle. Her neck was broken. It was my best friend, Antoinette, lying dead in the ditch. I screamed her name in despair. I heard a voice from afar calling for help. I turn my head toward the call. It was my brother stuck under the quad. As soon as I approached him, sensing my presence nearby, Justin lifted his head. His forehead was bleeding; his lips too. His skin was white, his lips were blue. The quad was lying on his stomach. I had two choices: either try to save my best friend and let my brother die, or try to save my brother and let my best friend die. I took a quick peek at Antoinette. She was still not moving. She already looked dead.

On the other hand, my brother was conscious and asking for help. I decided to save my brother. I tried to lift the quad. I couldn't lift it on my own, so I called Brandon to help me. He came running, along with Steven, to help me. Brandon and Steven were able to lift the quad while I pulled my brother out of there. Justin was severely injured, but he tried to stand up. I helped him stand. He was barely able to walk, but he started running and screaming anyway.

"Antoinette! Antoinette!"

Antoinette couldn't answer. She was dead.

I had seen enough. I couldn't see clearly; my eyes were full of tears. I walked up to Antoinette and cried, my head lying on her chest. I said to her loud and clear, "Antoinette, please forgive me. I love you with all my heart. I didn't have time to save you...if only I could turn back time..."

Antoinette's soul appeared in front of me and said, "I forgive you, Ashley. It was my time to go, not your brother's."

The images disappeared. I had cleared the simulated past. The serum wore off. The crowd was screaming and cheering. I didn't care. I was still crying. I ran off the chair. I just wanted to go to bed. I didn't want to see anybody, nor talk to anyone. What was Miss Grace thinking! How could she be so cruel! And Collin. And the world. I went to Mr. Hunter and said, "Permission to go to bed, please?"

"Sorry, no can do. Not until the tournament is done for the day. Those are the rules," Mr. Hunter replied.

Everybody came to pat me on the back and congratulate me, but I put my hand up in front of me to stop them.

"Not now. I just want to be alone."

They respected my wishes with sad and concerned faces.

"Well done, Ashley. Your time was two minutes and twenty-two seconds," said Miss Grace.

"Now, for the second chosen: Blake Clark from the Healing School," said Master Thunderstone.

The crowd went silent while they watched his simulation, like watching a movie. I didn't have the heart to look. It was such an invasion of his life that he didn't even have control of. I can't believe she had chosen this part of my life. The simulation was so manipulated, so wrong. I was lost in my thoughts when I heard Miss Grace say, "Well done, Blake. Your time was two minutes, fifty-eight seconds."

One hour later, the tournament was done for the day. I had finished first in this challenge, but I really didn't care. Collin was trying to carefully approach me, but I made sure not to look his way. As soon as the tournament was done, I teleported into my bedroom and went straight to bed. It was 8:04 p.m. I had just about two hours before my upcoming mission. I set my alarm for 9:45 p.m., and I took a nap, instantly falling into a deep sleep.

CHAPTER EIGHTEEN

I woke up at 9:40 p.m., before the alarm, from a recurring nightmare about Antoinette's death. I was all sweaty. I took a quick shower before teleporting to the Grounding School. All three teachers were already there, waiting for me.

"There you are. We were worried about you," said Miss Pomegrade.

I decided to ignore her comment and get down to business.

"You guys are all ready to go? You remember the plan?"

"Not before we know you are OK," said Collin.

I tried not to sound too harsh when I said, "I'm here and ready to go. I'm not here to socialize. We have business to do and then I'm going back to bed."

"Can I talk to you privately?" asked Collin.

"I'd rather not. There is nothing you can say to me that can't wait for another day. We have to get going, you guys."

Collin looked hurt. Miss Grace looked worried.

"Look, I'm sorry about the simulation. It obviously upset you. I had to—" said Miss Grace before I interrupted her.

"You went way out of line, and I can't believe you did that. If you are trying to hurt me, it's working. But I don't want to talk about it anymore, and honestly, I don't trust any of you right now. The faster we get this done, the faster I can move on and leave you all alone." I held onto cart full of the equipment we needed for the mission and said, "I will use the serum I created today to transport this across." I put a drop on the cart, and it went invisible. I drank the invisible serum and said, "I will see you on the other side. Get ready for your positions." Then I disappeared and left them speechless.

It didn't take them long to join me on the other side. Collin had to go in the building alone first to expose all the people inside the warehouse to the manipulation serum. He put on a mask and went inside. Within two minutes, a line of people was walking out of the building, following Collin. They were all looking straight ahead without talking. Collin led them into a bush nearby. As soon as the people were out of sight, us girls went in the warehouse. In the lab, we made a large portion of the antidote in a barrel. We then got the serum of destruction. We carefully emptied the gallons of the serum of destruction into several barrels, half full. We then added the antidotes for the remaining half. Miss Grace made sure to test the mixing with her ring before we went with the plan. Her ring stone turned green. It was good. We poured the useless serum of destruction back into its gallons and flasks. Then we repeated the same procedure with the lethal serum. It took two and a half hours to complete our mission. We took the invisibility serum again before we left the warehouse. Collin looked worried and annoyed that it had taken us so long. Collin drank the invisibility serum before manipulating the people to go back to their task. We waited for him outside the building. He had to erase the last three hours of the people's memory before heading back. As soon as he came back, we teleported to the Grounding School.

"What took you so long? I was worried sick and running out of ideas to keep the people occupied in the bush," said Collin.

"You try to add the antidote to every gallon and flask and see how time-consuming it is," said Miss Grace.

"Hopefully, it's going to work. I had an idea to go into Mr. Blake office and finish the mission, but maybe tomorrow night," I said.

"Tomorrow night isn't going to work. Just about everybody will be at the dance, and you will be noticed if you are not present. You left quite a signature at the tournament. Everybody is talking about you now," said Miss Grace.

"I think tomorrow will be the perfect time because the dance will be the distraction. Hear me out: I hate to dance, and I really don't care if I miss the dance," I tried.

"I'm going to stop you right there. You can't miss the dance. Besides, it's the best part of the tournament. Even the teachers are excited to go," said Miss Grace.

"Speak for yourself," said Collin. "Maybe we should listen to her idea before we decide on anything."

"Before I start, is it a requirement that the teachers attend the dance?"

"Well, I guess so," said Miss Pomegrade.

"No, it's not. I didn't go last year, and nothing happened to me," said Collin.

"OK, well, maybe Miss Grace can duplicate herself into me. That way nobody is going to notice my absence, and she will be able to dance all night and have all the attention she wants."

"You're forgetting that the serum lasts only an hour," said Miss Grace.

"You just have to watch the time and go to the bathroom to take another dose. I should be back by the second dose anyway. So in the meantime, Mr. Corrigan can duplicate into Mr. Blake while I will take the invisibility serum. That way I can help him with the antidote and spy to make sure no trouble appears without anybody seeing me. Mr. Corrigan will have to make sure to picture Mr. Blake in his work clothes with his security card tag on while he drinks the serum. I know the code for the safe."

"I like that plan," said Collin.

"There is only one problem. While I'm being Ashley, I can't be present at the dance, and that will be noticed. I normally dance all night at a party," said Miss Grace.

"I'll do it then. Nobody is going to notice my absence. I normally stay in a corner and watch the others dance," said Miss Pomegrade.

"Can you even dance?" asked Miss Grace.

"No."

"Good, because I can't dance either. My classmates know that. It will look funny if I danced all night anyway. Just make sure to act sick tomorrow. That way nobody will be too suspicious about your absence, in case somebody does notice it."

"Ashley, do you have a date for the dance?" asked Miss Pomegrade.

"Don't worry, I don't."

"But I don't have anything to wear at the dance," said Miss Pomegrade.

"I do. We will have to meet before. I will wear the dress. That way when you drink the serum, you will look at me and duplicate exactly the same as me. So everybody is on for tomorrow?"

"Yes, I'm in. What time should we do this?" asked Collin.

"The dance starts at 7 p.m. How about I meet Miss Pomegrade and you in the Warriors School at 6:45?"

"Sounds good," Collin and Miss Pomegrade replied.

"OK then, that settles it. Good night!" I teleported back into my bedroom before Collin could ask to talk to me again.

CHAPTER NINETEEN

"Good morning, wizards and witches. Today, for the final day of the tournament, the participants will have to face many challenges before attempting to steal the white flag. Only fifteen participants, three per devotion houses, are allowed to participate. The three participants will be the team's own choice. They will have to face challenges from each devotion house and more. The majority of the challenges will occur in a huge maze. There is only one rule: You can't teleport yourself out of the maze. Each participant is allowed to pick one object to bring in the maze. Of course, there are cameras all over the maze. We will be watching their performance. Once they are out of the maze, there will be a table full of other materials and serums. They will be able to serve themselves with whatever they need to get to the flag, no limitations. The first team that manages to steal the white flag will win this challenge. Devotion houses, prepare yourselves: You will have one minute to discuss and choose the three best participants and an additional minute to choose one item per person to take through the maze. Starting in one, two, three...now!"

We came to a circle. Everybody said, "Ashley, you are in."

"Very well. Mel is the strongest; he should be in too," I suggested.

"Agreed," they all said.

"Julius is fast and the best shooter," Mel added. Julius looked proud, and Stephany rolled her eyes.

"OK, that's three. Good luck! We're all counting on you," said Mr. Hunter. "You still have thirty seconds. I suggest you take a look at the items on the table and discuss your options."

We looked at the items. There were all kinds of things: water, mirrors, flashlights, knives, chains, food, bug sprays, torches, walking sticks, umbrellas, saws, Band-Aids, blankets, etc.

"OK, we have to think of what kind of challenges we are about to face in a maze and not choose the obvious like water and food," I said.

"I'm going to take a knife," said Julius.

"Good choice," I said.

"What should I take?" asked Mel.

"The fact that there are mirrors seems odd to me. I would choose that," I replied.

"What about a saw? Could be handy."

"Yes, but we have a knife that would do the same thing. A saw is too obvious. Bet you every team will have a saw," I replied.

"OK. What are you going to take?"

"A torch of course."

"Well, of course. A flashlight wouldn't do the trick," said Julius sarcastically.

"Oh, and let's choose last. We don't want any copy cats."

"Let me remind you that it's kind of a race," said Mel.

"Yes, I am aware of that. Something tells me that running won't make us win this race. Our skills and thinking will," I replied.

"Time's up. You have up to one minute to choose your items. As soon as your team has chosen the items, you are free to go in the maze. Good luck, everyone!" said Master Thunderstone.

Every team ran toward the table and picked one item as quickly as possible and started for the maze. The Warriors were the first ones in. They had taken a knife, a saw, and water. The Teleportation team had taken water, food, and bug spray. The Grounding team had taken water, food, and Band-Aids. The Healing team had taken water, flashlight, and a blanket. We took a mirror, a knife, and a torch.

As soon as we walked in, we heard screams on the left side. There were three paths, separated by tall, thick bushes. We saw footsteps on the right. The path straight ahead had a big snake looking at us.

"I am not taking this path. Let's take the right one," proposed Julius.

"No. That's the obvious way. Nobody took the straight path. Let's try it."

"But there is a snake!"

"I see that."

"Are you crazy? You go first."

I carefully approached the snake and started talking to it telepathically, like I used to do to any animal when I was a kid.

"Hey, pretty thing. How are you today?"

"Huh, aren't you supposed to be afraid of me?"

"Why would I be afraid of you? I like snakes!"

"Well, that's a first."

"What kind of snake are you anyway?"

"The kind that scares people away."

"Meaning?"

"They call me a Burmese python."

"Oh. So your diet is mostly birds and small mammals, right?"

"Correct. I also like little girls…"

I could tell he was just teasing me.

"Good thing I'm not little anymore then."

"Ha! Ha! Ha!" the snake laughed.

"Come on, guys. Walk by me. I'll stay near the python and protect you."

"Here, take my knife," said Julius.

"No need. Hurry, we don't have all day. May I remind you it's a race?" I teased them.

"Girl, you have some balls," said the snake.

"Well, one of us has to."

"Ha! Ha! Ha! Take a look at them! You would swear I was a monster or something!"

I laughed out loud.

"I don't see what's so funny," said Julius.

"You guys. It won't bite you!"

"But it could choke you to death."

"Right," I said sarcastically.

Once they had passed us, I said to the snake, "Well, I would love to stay and chat, but I got a race to go do."

"Good luck! Don't let the walls fool you."

"There, that wasn't so bad now, was it?" I asked the boys.

"I'll have nightmares tonight! That thing was huge!" said Julius.

"Enough time wasted. Let's run," said Mel.

They started running. I had no choice but to follow. The path became muddier by the minute, until it was thick, wet sand, the size of a little farm pond, in front of us.

"Wait! Stop!" I screamed.

"What is it?" asked Mel.

"Looks like quicksand," I replied.

"There's only one way to find out," Mel said. He took a rock and threw it in the wet sand. It sunk right away.

"I guess we are on the wrong path. Let's turn around," said Mel.

"Great! I don't know if I can face the snake again!" said Julius.

"Guys! Are you wizards or not?"

"Yes, but that's out of our league."

"No, it's not. We just have to teleport to the other side of the quicksand pond."

"Right," they both replied.

I was the first to teleport.

"Come on, it's safe!"

They teleported one at a time. We continued down the path. We came to a tunnel. It was pitch black, and we couldn't see anything. We could hear and feel bats flying around us. Julius was freaked out. I opened the torch. The fire scared away the bats.

"Good call, Ashley," said Mel.

"Yeah, Julius here was about to pee in his pants," I said.

"Pfff," denied Julius.

"Good one," said Mel.

The sun appeared again. We could see the sky, so I turned off the torch.

"You know, I used to like you, Ash, but now..." Julius stopped dead. He looked straight in front of him.

Right in front of us was a bloody girl, begging for me to help her. It was Antoinette. I wouldn't let it get to me this time. I said out loud, "You know, Antoinette, I already asked you many times to forgive me, and you already forgave me more than once. I am ready to let you go and move on with my life. I forgive myself for what happened. What do you say? It's time for you to go to heaven where you belong! The angels are waiting for you. I no longer need you here, but you will always remain in my heart."

Antoinette smiled and waved at me before she disappeared. I was a bit shaken at seeing her, she looked so real, but I didn't let it get to me. We had to get out of this maze as quickly as possible. A little boy appeared in front of us, crying. I didn't know this boy, but from the look on Mel's face, I knew he knew who it was met for. Mel didn't move. He was startled by seeing this boy.

"Who is it, Mel?" I asked.

"It's my little brother."

"Why is he crying?"

"Probably because I left him alone in the park when I should have been watching over him. He got stung by a bee and died at five years old. I was too busy playing catch with my friend, and I didn't see him."

"Did you ask him for forgiveness?" I asked.

"Well, no. When I found him, he was already dead."

"Well, maybe it's time you let him know now."

Mel approached his brother and got on his knees. He had tears in his eyes. He said to him, "Cole, I am so sorry. I didn't see what happened to you. I should have been on your side. You're my little brother. I never wanted you to die."

Cole gave him a hug and disappeared. An orange cat appeared in front of us. It was Julius's time to deal with this. Julius just stood there with his mouth awkwardly open.

"Julius, whatever you did to this cat, I think you owe it an apology," I said.

"But it's a cat!"

"Cats have feelings and souls too, you know."

Julius approached the cat. Its fur went up, and it started hissing at him.

"Hey, Garfield. Um, I'm sorry about throwing rocks at you, cutting your tail, and feeding you poison when I was a kid. It was cruel and wrong of me. I didn't really want you dead; I was just trying to impress my neighbor. Please forgive me."

"I will forgive you on one condition—pet me like a normal kid would."

Of course, Julius didn't hear what the cat said.

"Julius, show your love by petting him."

Julius gave me an odd look but did it anyway. Garfield disappeared.

We walked silently, side by side, for the next few minutes. Suddenly, some branches grabbed my ankles. I fell to the ground. I tried to untie my ankles, but other branches grabbed my arms and torso.

"Julius! Your knife!"

Julius and Mel both jumped on the branches. Julius tried to cut the branches with the knife while Mel grabbed one piece of branch going for my neck and pulled as hard as he could. The knife was only sharp enough to cut branches one at a time. By the time all the moving branches had been cut, we were all exhausted and out of breath. We couldn't run anymore, but we walked as fast as we could. We were very thirsty. It was overly warm all of a sudden. We were sweating bullets. A wasp nest fell right in front of us, leaving a cloud of mad wasps coming our way. I quickly opened the torch and lit the cloud on fire. It killed many wasps and scared away the rest. I was even warmer with the fire open, but I didn't kill the fire until all the wasps were gone.

"I need water. Water would have been nice just about now," said Julius. "We are the only team that didn't pick water."

"Maybe I should have taken water instead of the useless mirror," said Mel.

There was a big flowerbed in front of us. Something caught my eye. Mint. I grabbed three leaves and smelled them to make sure it was really mint before I gave them each a leaf.

"Suck on this. It should relieve your thirst," I said.

We did. The effect was instant—the thirst was gone.

"Thanks," said Mel.

We eventually came to another three-way intersection. On our left, we heard people screaming for help. We looked at each other. I said, "We can't leave them like this. They need our help."

"Since when do we help our opponents?" said Julius.

"Ashley, it could be another trap, a simulation of some kind," suggested Mel.

"Or it could be classmates who are in real danger. I'm taking the chance."

I turned my back and started running toward the screams. My teammates had no choice but to follow me this time. We recognized the Healing team; all three of them were stuck to their neck in quicksand.

Mel broke a branch nearby and said to the first girl, "Here, hold on to this stick, and I'll try to pull you out. Come on, you two. Do the same."

Julius went to look for another branch. Mel used all his strength but couldn't pull the girl out. He eventually slipped and fell in the sand. Julius immediately dove and grabbed both of his arms and tried to pull him out. He was sinking fast. Julius was starting to slide toward the sand.

"Ashley! Do something!" screamed Mel.

I put my hand up toward the girl and made her fly out of the sand. I did the same to the other two opponents and finally to Mel. They were all covered in mud from head to toe and out of breath.

"How did you do that?" asked Julius, amazed.

"It's called teleportation of objects. Ever heard of it?" I teased him.

"Thanks, Ash," said Mel.

"Yeah, thanks," said our opponents.

"Look at us! It's the dance tonight! It will never come off," said the girl.

"I heard it's good for the skin," I tried.

"Never mind the mud. Look, I'm covered in wasp bites!" said Karl. He was right; he was covered everywhere.

"Look at the bright side. The mud will help heal your bites," I said.

"They dumped a nest on you too?" asked Julius.

"Yes, it was terrible. This whole maze is a nightmare. I should have never volunteered," said Karl

"Hey, guys, I would love to chat but—" I stopped. Right in front of us was a tiger.

"Holy shit!" said Karl.

The girl and Julius started screaming. The tiger roared even louder.

"OK, calm down, guys. It's just a tiger," I said.

"Just a tiger! What are you talking about, just a tiger?" said Franklin.

I took a few steps toward the tiger and said telepathically, "Hey, cutie, what are you doing?"

"Scaring the shit out of you humans."

"Really? I'm not afraid of you. I love tigers. They are my favorite animals."

"Today is your lucky day then, little girl, because it's the last thing you are going to see."

"Oh, come on. Don't be like that."

"Watch me."

The tiger roared just a few inches from my face and then raked his claws over my arm. I was bleeding, but I would take care of that later.

"Mel? Try to blind the tiger with the mirror and the sun. What's your name again...Jackie?" I said, all the while keeping my eyes on the tiger.

"Yes."

"Jackie, when Mel blinds the tiger, throw the blankets on its head. Don't miss. Julius, when the blanket is on its head, take your knife and stab its paw. I will burn the other one. Ready?"

No response, but I gave the countdown anyway: "One, two, three."

Mel put up the mirror and tried to reflect the sun in its eyes. It took him a few seconds before he could aim at its eyes. The tiger was blinded and looked away.

"Now, Jackie!"

Jackie threw the blanket on its head.

I lit the torch and said, "Hurry, Julius. On three: one, two, three!"

Julius stabbed its right paw while I burned his left paw.

"Run!" I ordered.

We ran and ran until we came back to the intersection. The Grounding team was at the intersection, debating which path to take. When they saw us, they all stopped talking and just stared at us.

"If you want a chance to live, give me your food, Simon."

He looked at me like I was mad. But once he saw that we were serious, he gave it to me. I took it and threw it as far as possible to the far end of the right path.

"Follow us!" I screamed, running backward.

They looked at us with puzzled looks. When they heard the roar approaching, they decided to run with us. We eventually heard the roar going farther and farther away. We slowed down, out of breath.

"It probably smelled the food and went for it," I said.

"I sure hope you're right," said Jackie.

"What happened to you guys?" asked Mel.

The Grounding team were covered in cuts and Band-Aids.

"Some carnivorous plant attacked us," said Simon.

"Geez! What else are we going to find?" said Franklin.

"I don't know, but let's get out of here," I proposed.

"Amen!" said Julius.

"Hey, Ashley, you are bleeding!" said Mel.

"Oh, that! It's nothing! I'm fine."

"No, it's not fine. The tiger attacked you!" said Jackie.

"Really, I'm fine. Plus, we don't have time to stop."

The nine of us walked together as one team. I started to secretly heal my arm. We came to a mirror maze. It was hypnotizing and confusing. We couldn't find the path. We kept bumping into the mirrored walls. We were all holding hands.

"Mel, use your mirror to find the path, and whoever has the flashlight, use that too."

Karl and Mel used their respective items to find the way through the mirrored maze. On the other side of the mirrored maze was a little lake.

Jackie, Karl, Franklin, and Mel ran in it to wash the mud away. It didn't take long for them to realize that the lake was full of leeches. Jackie screamed. The others were just as freaked out. They were doing the chicken dance, trying to shake them off. I opened my torch again and said to them, "Stay very still." They froze. I put the flame close to the leeches. The leeches couldn't handle the heat, and they fell one by one to the ground.

After, they thanked me and Julius said, "Now how will we cross the lake?"

"Dah! Teleportation!" I said.

"Right!"

"But I still can't teleport!" said Jackie.

"Hold my hand. I'll make you teleport," I said.

Once we were all across the lake, we came to the only way out of the maze. We could see the stands and spectators from here. The Warrior and the Teleportation teams were already there, losing patience. There was a gate, but the only way to open the gate was to find the answer to the enigma. Any attempt to touch the gate gave them an electric shock.

"This is bullshit! We've been here for half an hour already. This is the worst tournament ever," screamed Steven.

"So what's the enigma?" I asked.

"I told you, it's impossible to find. We've tried for half an hour. The Teleportation team was here fifteen minutes ago, and they can't find it either. Now back off. We were here first."

"I used to do enigmas all the time when I was a kid. Let me try," I dared.

"Suit yourself. But if you find it, which you won't, you are still at the end of the line. Got it?"

"Yup!"

He read the enigma out loud: "*I never was, am always to be, no one ever saw me, nor ever will, and yet I am the confidence of all to live and breathe on this terrestrial ball. What am I?*"

"Well, that's easy!" said Julius. "It's God."

"No, it's not. We tried that already," said Steven.

"I know what it is. Where do I say the answer to make the gate open?" I asked.

"Press this button and speak loud. You seem pretty confident. Just so you know, if it's the wrong answer, you will get electrified. That should be funny. Back up, everybody," said Steven.

"Oh, is that what happened to your brain? Too many wrong answers?" I replied.

"Ha! Ha! Ha! Good one," said Mel. Everybody else tried not to laugh, but Joshua, from his own team, almost choked laughing.

I pressed the button and said out loud, "The answer is tomorrow." The gate unlocked. Everybody, except Steven of course, cheered and tapped me on the shoulder. The crowd went wild. They were screaming, "Ashley! Ashley!" Steven pushed me aside and ran out of the maze, followed by his teammates. Then the Teleportation team ran out followed by the Grounding team, the Healing team and finally us. We all came to a halt when we saw what was ahead of us. There, in front of us, was a huge, furious, and, thank God, tied-up multicolored dragon with big wings and a pointy tail. It had sharp, bony bumps like a stegosaurus on his back and big bright yellow eyes. I immediately said to myself, "So that was the big roar I heard behind the bush and the reasons for the gun shots and injuries and the burned man." The flag was on top of a hill behind the dragon. To our right was a table full of items we could use. We all went to the table. All three of the warriors had a sword in hand and were getting ready for a plan of attack. Steven was being a coward again; he was letting Joshua and Brad go first and attack the dragon while he would go steal the flag. Joshua walked slowly toward the dragon, trying to distract it. The dragon immediately went for Joshua and spit fire. Joshua teleported away, avoiding the fire by just inches. The crowd was getting nervous. Brad went the opposite way. The dragon saw him and turned Brad's way. Its big tail knocked Joshua down, and he hit his head hard on a big rock. He was lying on the ground, unconscious. The dragon spit fire on Brad. His hat caught on fire. Brad had the reflexes to take his hat off and throw it on the ground. He ran as fast as he could back to the starting point, out of reach of the dragon. The dragon got mad trying to reach for Brad, but its chain was holding him back. I tried to reason with the dragon telepathically.

"Hey, can you turn it down a notch? If you behave, maybe they will free you. Misbehave, and you will remain chained for the rest of your life."

He savagely roared at me, saying that he was hungry and needed fresh flesh and that he didn't care about his future. The more killing he could do, the merrier he would be. He wanted his revenge for capturing him like a prisoner for so long. I knew there was nothing I could say to reason with him. I said to Mel, "Go to the right, but stay out of reach of the dragon. Try to distract him. I'll go help Joshua," I said.

Mel went to the right with the mirror still in its hand. It caught the dragon's attention. He tried to blind it with the reflection of the sun. But the dragon was so high, Mel had trouble aiming at its eyes. Nevertheless, the dancing bright light was distracting the dragon. I teleported to Joshua's side. I tried to lift him, but he was too heavy. I pulled him behind the big rock, sheltered from the dragon's reach and flames. I noticed he was bleeding from his skull. I put my hand above his head and healed his wound. While I was working on Joshua, Julius teleported behind the big rock and told me he was going for the flag. Before I could deny anything, he teleported for the flag but hit an invisible wall. He was instantly knocked down and went unconscious too. The dragon heard the knocking noise and saw

Julius. He was running toward Julius. His mind told me he was going to spit fire at him. Acting with instinct, I put a protective shield around Julius and directed the flames to the left. This caught the dragon by surprise, and he tried harder. I directed the flames toward the dragon this time and burned his eyes. While the dragon was blinded for a moment and raging in pain, I pulled Julius beside Joshua. I could see that Julius's collarbone was broken. I attended to his injury and tried to heal him. Steven took advantage of the situation and tried to run toward the flag. The dragon sensed the motion and grabbed Steven by his hoodie and swung him from side to side. Steven was screaming his lungs off, and the crowd stood up, holding their breath. Even the teachers couldn't believe what was happening. I made a sword from the table fly toward the dragon's jaw. It pierced one side of it. The dragon opened his mouth to scream and let go of the hoodie. Steven fell down. I made the fall stop just inches off the ground and tried something new. I tried to make Steven tele-port back to the table, just like an object. It worked. I did the same to Joshua, then to Julius. Doctors came running to pick up both Joshua and Julius and rush them to the hospital. Steven looked at me in disbelief. He couldn't believe I had just saved him, after all he had done to me. He walked back to his partner, not before nodding at me. It was more than I could ask. I nodded back to him.

Mel came running to me and said, "Good move, Ashley! What's next?"

"There is obviously an invisible wall, maybe like a window, around the flag. We need to break it if we have any chance at stealing the flag," I said.

"Yeah, but how?"

"Like this."

I made all of the swords fly toward the flag as fast as I could. The swords shattered the crystal clear window into thousands of pieces. Steven didn't wait a second. He teleported toward the flag. Just before he reached the flag, Steven got zapped and fell to the ground.

"Shit. Another protective shield," I said.

The dragon was about to step down and crush Steven when I made him teleport back to the table. Steven was still conscious, but his whole body was shaking uncontrollably. His hands were burned pretty badly. I had to act quickly before the nurses came to attend to Steven. I put my hand toward Steven's heart. He stopped shaking shortly after. Steven looked at me with frightened eyes. He started moaning, "My hands! Ah! They hurt so much!"

I took his hands into mine. He screamed, "Ah! Don't touch me! Ah!" But before he knew it, his hands were healed. He looked at his hands in disbelief and whispered to me, "What are you?"

"You know what I am," I replied before I turned my back on him and joined Mel. Only, I knew he had no clue of what I was...even I had no clue. The only thing I knew was that I was a powerful, gifted person. Deep down inside I knew I was not a witch.

"What just happened, Ash?" asked Mel.

"Nothing."

The sun was so bright. I lifted my face up, closed my eyes, and breathed it in. It felt so good on my skin. When I opened my eyes again, something caught my eye. At the very top of the dome, above the dragon, was a huge metal cage. I tried to make it move and trap the dragon, but it was bolted to the ceiling. I remembered there was a welding torch on the table. I grabbed it. Before I left, I whispered to Mel, "Wear the rubber boots, raincoat, hat, and gloves. There is only one pair of each. As soon as the dragon is trapped in the cage, teleport fast to the flag and grab it.

The rubber should protect you from the zapping." He looked at me with an unsure look. "Trust me," I said. He nodded.

I teleported to the top of the cage. With one hand I used the torch to melt the bolt chains. The dragon spit fire toward me, but I had put a protective shield around me, and the flames deviated. I could hear the "Ooohs and Aaaahs" from the crowd. I could hear Steven ordering Brad to go steal the flag while the dragon wasn't looking. Brad refused to try. Within five minutes, the chains were unbolted. I made the cage move and managed to trap the dragon under it. I bolted the chains to the ground and screamed "Now, Mel!" Mel teleported, grabbed the flag, and swung it in the air. The crowd went wild. We heard the Master's voice say, "And the winner of this year's tournament is the Formula School!"

My whole devotion house came running in the stadium and hugged me, swinging me in the air. Even Mr. Hunter was smiling from ear to ear. The crowd was screaming my name. I could tell that this bothered Master Thunderstone. He had witnessed my unusual powers without a ring and decided that I was a threat for the island, for his kingdom. He was the most powerful wizard in the world, and he wanted to keep it that way. He couldn't let a young lady get more and more powerful and have all the love and attention he longed for. He wanted to get rid of me as soon as possible, without attracting attention or suspicion. The more people loved me, the bigger threat I was. He started to regret ignoring Seth's warning about me. I could have been dead by now, without getting his hands dirty.

All the remaining participants came in the middle of the stadium, and we shook hands. They all said "Good game" to me, including the teachers. When Collin shook my hand, he said telepathically to me, "Good job Ash, but watch your back. You're in danger. Stay in public places. Don't even go in your room alone."

"Ashley! You were awesome! I'm so glad you are in our devotion house. You truly are an inspiration. Thank you so much for saving Joshua. He means the world to me. I owe you so much. If there is anything I can do for you, let me know," said Veronica.

"Actually, there is. After the distribution of the medals, could you come into my room with me and help me get ready? I have no clue how to do my hair for the dance."

"Absolutely! I would be honored."

CHAPTER TWENTY

"You are absolutely gorgeous!" said Veronica. I looked in the mirror. She had put my hair up and left some of it down with curls. What a difference it made from what I normally looked like! The dress brought out my bright blue eyes. She had lent me some earrings and a necklace that matched my dress. She had put some blue nail polish on my fingernails and toenails for me. She was wearing a black-and-hot pink dress with pink high-heeled shoes. She looked stunning. She had put some waves in her long black hair, and with all of her makeup, she looked much older.

"You look amazing yourself. I'm sure Joshua won't be able to take his eyes off you."

"Thanks, Ash. I hope he will show up to the dance. I hope he's OK."

"I'm sure he is," I said.

I looked at my watch. It was 6:42.

"Well, shall we go? I'm so excited," Veronica said.

"I just need to powder my nose first. I'll be right back."

I locked the bathroom door and teleported to the Warriors School. Miss Pomegrade and Collin were already there. Collin whistled when he saw me.

"My, my, Ashley. Look at you! You're stunning!" said Miss Pomegrade.

"Indeed," said Collin.

"Thanks. Miss Pomegrade, Veronica is waiting in my room. You will go to the dance with her. You will have to teleport to my bathroom."

She drank the duplicate serum and teleported to my bathroom.

Collin leaned toward me to kiss me. I took a step back.

"We need to get going. Drink this and think of Mr. Blake in his suit with the security card on him."

"You look amazing, Ashley. We don't even have a time for a little kiss?"

"No. Hurry. We don't have all night."

"You are so bossy," he said before drinking the duplicate serum.

It was impressive to see Mr. Blake right in front of me.

"Well? How do I look?" asked Collin.

"Like Mr. Blake. Try to use a deeper, lower voice if you need to talk."

"You truly are stunning, Ashley. Like this?"

"Much better. OK, off we go." I grabbed the bag with the antidote serum and drank the invisible serum.

We teleported right in front of the building.

"Try to act normal. You look nervous."

"Easy for you to say. You're invisible."

It was true. Nobody could see me, but they could hear my high heels. I took them off and hid them in the flowerbed. Collin swiped his card, and the door unlocked. I knew which way to go, but Collin didn't. The fact that he couldn't see me to follow me caused a problem. I had forgotten this little detail. Talking would be too risky. I took his arm, leaned to his ear, and whispered, "You have to go through security to pass. Then keep going straight. I'll catch up."

I could see sweat coming down his temples.

"Mr. Blake? I thought you were done for the day. Didn't you have an important meeting to attend to with the Master?" asked the security guy.

"Yes, forgot a document in the office. I'll be in and out."

"Are you OK, Mr. Blake? You look troubled. Are you sick? Your voice seems rough."

"Just allergies."

"Allergies? Since when do you have allergies?"

"Since always. Just forgot to take my medicine today."

"Would you like me to find some for you?"

"No, thanks. Look, I'm in a hurry. Master is waiting for me."

"Say no more. Come through," said the guard.

He passed the scanner with no problems. Me, I had to squeeze in between the gate and the scanner without being noticed. My bag got stuck. My bottle of water fell on the ground. It didn't go unnoticed.

"Huh?" said the guard. He picked it up and looked confused. "Where did this come from?"

"It must have been Mr. Blake's."

"Hey, Mr. Blake?"

Collin stopped. "Yes?"

"Is this your bottle of water?"

"Oh, yes. Thanks."

"Do you mind if we scan it? You know the protocol."

"Go ahead."

They scanned it.

"OK. You are good to go."

I took the bag and quickly joined Collin. I took his arm back.

"That was a close one," he said to me.

"Yeah!" I replied. "First right, second door on your left-hand side." He scanned the door. I ran in and punched in the code to the safe. The door opened. "Now follow my instructions to the letter while I stand guard in the hallway.

"How many flasks?" I asked

"Ten."

"OK. Carefully pour the ten flasks into the pot in the bag." I waited for him to follow my instructions. A couple of minutes later he responded.

"Done."

"Now add ten cups of the antidotes and mix it."

"Done," he said.

"Make sure the antidote succeeded with your ring before pouring it back into the flasks. Pour the rest in the jar and seal it."

He did as he was told. He was just about to finish pouring the antidote into the flasks when I heard footsteps running toward us.

"We have company. Hurry...sounds like an army is running our way."

The first face I saw turning the corner was the angry face of Mr. Blake.

"It's Mr. Blake! We are busted. Drink the invisibility serum." I pulled a table and placed it in front of the door. "Make it look like a burglary. I'll take it from here with the flask."

He looked at me with a questioning look, but we didn't have time to discuss it. He drank the invisibility serum and started to open the files on the desk and search in the drawers while I put everything back into the safe box, closed it, and armed it. Mr. Blake and his guards were banging on the door savagely, trying to force it open. When they managed to open the door halfway, the first thing Mr. Blake saw was his identical twin searching in his files. He was shocked and didn't move for a few seconds. Then he took out his gun and shot at Collin just before he disappeared in front of his eyes.

"What? Where did he go? I shot him and now he's gone!" screamed Mr. Blake.

When they managed to move the table away and walk into his office, they searched everywhere for Collin.

"Look! There is blood on the floor!" said a guard.

Collin had been shot on the shoulder. I helped him out of the office, and we started running toward the exit. We managed to squeeze in between the gate and the scanner easily this time. Outside the entrance door were guards. We were stuck. There was no other way out. There was no window accessible without the proper security card. We had to get out through the exit door.

"We need to get out. I'll put a protective shield around us. As soon as we are out, we have to teleport back into your school. We can't teleport anywhere from inside this building. On three. One, two, three!"

We opened the door. The guards couldn't see anyone, but they started shooting at us anyway. The bullets lodged into the ground. Collin and I teleported back into the Warriors School. I immediately started to heal his shoulder.

"Sorry, Collin. Lay on the table here. I need to take the bullet out of your shoulder before I can heal it. Stay very still...Oh, and bite on this." I gave him a pen to bite on while I took the bullet out with a knife. Collin was writhing in pain. He had turned back into himself; the serum had worn off on both of us all too soon. Once the bullet was out, I placed my hand on his shoulder and started to heal it. It didn't take too long.

"What a disaster!" said Collin.

"Yeah. But we need to get back to the dance. Security will be at the max now, and every absence will be noted.

"Agreed."

Drinking another dose of invisible serum, Collin and I went to the cafeteria where the dance was occurring. We didn't quite find the ambiance we were expecting. Nobody was dancing. Everybody was whispering to each other. "Ashley" was nowhere to be found. Someone was approaching us. It was Miss Grace.

"What's going on, Miss Grace?" I whispered.

Miss Grace jumped, startled.

"What are you doing here? You can't be exposed. Come hide behind the curtains." Miss Grace was standing in front of the curtains, talking to us telepathically. "Collin and Miss Pomegrade's absence have been already noticed. They are searching for you."

"Why? And where is Ashley...I mean, Miss Pomegrade?" Mr. Corrigan asked.

"They arrested and captured Ashley during the dance."

"For what?" I asked.

"For spying and breaching the wizards."

"That's nonsense," I said.

"They even said that if someone else is missing, they will kill an innocent every hour until someone speaks or turns themselves in. Collin and Miss Pomegrade are accused of being your allies. I heard they will terminate you tonight."

"Oh, my God! What are we going to do?" asked Collin.

"We have to go to the jail and find Miss Pomegrade before they kill her," I said.

"Yes, but how?" asked Collin.

Mr. Hunter walked by Miss Grace.

"Any luck?" asked Mr. Hunter.

"No, pretty quiet on this side."

"You walk toward the right; I'll take the left side. They have to be here. There is nowhere to hide."

Miss Grace walked away from us, leaving Collin and I alone behind the curtains.

"Let's go to the jail. I'll think of something once we are there."

"This is insane!"

"Collin, I can't let them kill Miss Pomegrade because of me. You don't have to come, but I am going."

"Do you really think I'm going to let you go alone? I have to protect my sunshine."

We teleported in front of the jail. We knew the jail had a protective shield around it to prevent any teleportation activities in and out. There were two guards stationed at the front door and two more on the roof.

"Do you still have the manipulation serum?"

"It's hiding in my locker at school. Why?"

"We need it. By exposing the guards, they can let us enter and lead us to Miss Pomegrade."

"Good thinking. I'll go get it."

"No need. Just make it teleport it here."

"Right."

"Might as well teleport two hygiene masks too so we don't breathe it."

He did. We walked toward the guards and infused them with the serum, protected by the masks on our faces. Collin gave them orders.

"Open the door. Bring me to Ashley's cell."

The guards opened the door with a blank look. They walked toward the cells. Ashley's cell was empty. The guards looked confused. Collin asked them to find out where she was. As they were walking like robots down the hallway, the head security guard said, "What are you two doing here? Get back to your station now!"

Collin whispered in their ears what they should say. "We just want to make sure that Ashley didn't escape. Master ordered maximum security...just making sure..."

"Enough of this bullshit! She can't escape, and you know it. Pretty soon she will be history. Now get back!"

"Well, where is she? She's not in her cell..."

"What do you care? She's in the termination room. Now you have five seconds to get back to your station or I will shoot you. Do I make myself clear?"

I ordered the two guards to go back. I noticed a map on the wall. Termination room was in room C142. I showed it to Collin, and we ran toward the termination room. There was no window in the steel door or the walls. It was total silence. Running out of ideas, I knocked on the door. Nothing. I kicked the door the second time. Someone opened the door halfway and said, "Do you mind? We are in a middle of something." He stopped. There was nobody at the door. He looked both ways in the hallway. I leaned near his ear and said, "Boooo!" He jumped and let the door open. We entered. Ashley was duct taped to a chair. She had duct tape on her mouth and tears running down her cheeks. She looked frightened. At the sight of her, it gave me goosebumps. I could tell it affected Collin too. Collin jumped at the cop and started punching him while I untied Miss Pomegrade. There was obviously an invisible wall window in the room because two men came running in the room and shot Miss Pomegrade in the head and the stomach. She was instantly dead. My arm got hit too in the savage shooting. Ashley's dead body retransformed into Miss Pomegrade. That freaked out the cops, and the shooting stopped. I ran to Miss Pomegrade and tried to heal her. Her wounds slowly closed, but it was already too late. When I saw her spirit looking at her body, I screamed "No!"

In anger and in pain, I was unable to move while looking at my friend's dead body when Collin grabbed me by the arm and guided us out of the building before he teleported us to the Warriors School.

People were waiting for Collin there, so we teleported to the Grounding School. There were people waiting at every school. So I decided to teleport to the secret area of the storage room. I couldn't stop crying. I couldn't get Miss Pomegrade's dead body off my mind. Collin kissed me on the head and hugged me. Then he said, "Can you heal your arm before the blood reveals our whereabouts?"

CHAPTER TWENTY-ONE

I healed my arm, then I screamed, "It should have been me, not her!"

"This should never have happened, not to you or anybody. This was out of our control!" said Collin, trying to keep his cool.

"Was it? 'Cause it seems pretty obvious to me none of this would have happened without me."

"We took a chance. It was a good plan, but things got twisted, that's all. Remember that she agreed to take the risk. She died with honor, like a true soldier. Now I need you to calm down and focus. We will have time to mourn once everything is done. We have to find a way to escape form this island or they will find us and kill us. We can't keep on taking the invisible serum forever."

I knew he was right. But something popped into my mind. "We can't escape just now. They saw that they killed Miss Pomegrade, not me, just like they saw the double of Mr. Blake before you disappeared. They will know that we had a plan. They will not trust anybody. They will try anything in their power to find out what the plan was. Every teacher and every member of the Formula devotion will be their first target until they discover what they can. We can't abandon them. We need to fight them and fix it."

"Spoken like a true warrior. Amen. But we are just two against an army of wizards. Let's be realistic here."

"Then let's recruit a secret army, only people we can trust. We can read people's minds, shouldn't be too hard to find. We need to destroy the supplies storage building."

"And kill all the bad wizards," continued Collin.

"I don't know about that. Killing is not my thing."

"OK, then let's recruit an army and divide in two, one half with you destroying the storage and finding a way off the island while my half goes to war."

"OK. Let's find Miss Grace first. She can convince more people by being visible than invisible."

"Good point."

We drank another dose of invisibility serum and teleported back into the cafeteria. We found Grace, still near the curtains. We went to her and said in her ear, "We need to talk." She jumped but then walked into a corner, away from the crowd. We explained what had happened and what we intended to do.

"So how are we supposed to recruit anyone? We are being watched, and you two are the most wanted people on this island. You can't be seen. Someone is bound to discover you."

"Collin and I can read people's minds. We will know if a certain person is worthy of trust."

"But nobody can see you. You can't just walk by and talk to people. You are invisible!"

"No, but you can be our voice. We will be by your side. We will let you know if we can't trust someone."

"And don't get any crazy ideas about trying to recruit secret agents and government people," said Collin.

"I wasn't going to," Miss Grace responded hurtfully.

She informed us that they had killed Justin, Joshua's brother, because the Master was mad when he found out Ashley was still alive. "They asked us to please come forward if we had any ideas of her whereabouts."

"I bet you Joshua will want revenge, that we could count on him," I said.

"You are right. I'm sure he would," said Collin.

"And I'm sure we can count on Veronica, Mel, and Julius," I added.

"I have a few old friends I could try to persuade," said Miss Grace.

"What kind of old friends?" asked Collin.

"The kind nobody would pay attention to. They are the stay-at-home moms who are not working, still raising their kids. I know a few guys too who I used to date before they settled down and got married," said Miss Grace.

"Are you sure that would be wise?"

"Are you judging me?" said Miss Grace.

"No, it's just that moms raising kids won't want to go to war," replied Collin.

"He does have a point," I added.

"We need to focus on the people who have guts, who are mad and confident," said Collin.

"I think Miss Travel would do anything to get out of here," I said.

"You got that right. But cross Mr. Hunter out...even though he owes you the gold medal," said Collin.

"What about the girl you dated with red hair?" asked Miss Grace.

"I'm sure she would, but she's not on this island, so forget it," he replied.

"OK, so how do we go about recruiting people without being noticed?" asked Miss Grace.

Master Thunderstone walked into the cafeteria. It didn't take long before there was total silence. He took his ring and spoke with an authoritative voice.

"We are temporally in a crisis. Like any crisis, changes must be made until everything falls back to normal. Our island has been compromised. Ashley Connors is a wicked witch trying to take over this island and destroy it. We have reasons to believe that Mr. Corrigan and Miss Pomegrade were her allies. We thought we had captured her and terminated her before she could terminate us one by one. Unfortunately, Miss Pomegrade was disguised as Ashley at the time of the capture," said Master Thunderstone.

" The real Ashley and Mr. Corrigan are still on this island, hiding. We strongly suggest that anyone who has an idea of their whereabouts should please come forward to me in private and your identity will remain anonymous," he continued.

"Ashley is extremely powerful with unusual and unique powers. If you witness something that seems odd, please report it to the authorities. If you come across Ashley, or Mr. Corrigan, please act as normal as possible and avoid talking to them. Let me remind you that they are extremely dangerous and that they are not to be trusted. Unexpected events created chaos among authorities. I fear that there may be more allies among them in this room," stressed Master Thunderstone.

"To prevent any secret forces against the authority or a revolution, we will abolish the five devotion house for the moment, until advised otherwise. Instead, we will temporary unite all five devotions together, mixing the students in separate houses, supervised. It is not the time to make friends with anybody. It is not the time to trust anyone. Just know that the authorities will do everything in their power to keep you safe, assured Master Thunderstone.

"There will be curfews; nobody should be walking outside their new devotion house past 7 p.m. At no time should you be walking alone. School hours will be the same. We will provide you with your new schedule tomorrow morning. Mr. Seth Dawson will be Mr. Corrigan's replacement, and Miss Bubbles will be Miss Pomegrade's replacement. The Grounding and the Healing Schools will be temporary closed because we will team up the teachers for better protection and supervision. I will have a small meeting with the teachers to establish the new teams, and we will thereafter divide the students. Teachers, let's meet at the back table in two minutes," asked the Master.

We could hear murmurs of surprise and worry in the room.

"Try to team up with Miss Travel" I said to Grace.

"Yeah, my favorite person in the whole world," she replied.

"We'll be right next to you. Pay attention to our instructions," said Collin.

The teachers gathered together at the back table.

211 Child of The Sun

"OK, there' are going to be three teams: Seth will be with Mr. Blake in the Warriors School. Then there will be a pair of teachers at the Formula School and a pair of teachers in the Teleportation School. Any suggestions?" asked Master Thunderstone.

"I'm going to have to request to not team up with Miss Travel because we have our differences and it would be impossible for me to work with her," said Mr. Hunter.

I could read the Master's mind that he was going to disregard his request. He didn't want any bonding between teachers. I said to Grace telepathically, "Tell him you don't want to work with her either. Tell him you can't stand her and that she's just a lazy hypocrite who stabs everybody in the back."

"What?" she replied.

"Just do it."

"With all due respect, Master, I don't think I could work with her either. We have never been friends since we were kids. I can't stand the thought to be stuck with her. She is nothing but a lazy hypocrite who stabs everybody in the back..."

Miss Travel's mouth dropped. She was hurt. It was true that they were not the best of friends, but to say a comment like that was unfair.

"Well in that case, you're exactly the person I need to keep her in line, Miss Grace. **You** will team up with her," ordered Master Thunderstone.

"Now how should we divide the students? I don't want handpicks. I don't want your opinion of any students," said Master Thunderstone.

"Propose alphabetical order," I said.

"How about in alphabetical order?" Miss Grace proposed.

"Good idea. A to G will be with Miss Grace and Miss Travel, H to M with Mr. Hunter and Miss Bubbles, and N to Z with Seth and Blake. That settles it."

Collin looked at me with a puzzled face. I told him, "You will see."

CHAPTER TWENTY-TWO

In the recreation room of the original Teleportation School, the students were all assembled. Miss Grace had called a meeting. Standing invisible in front of the crowd, I recognized most of the students and was pleased with the recruits. There before me were Joshua, Veronica, Mel, Julius, Karl, Jackie, Franklin, Simon, Brad, Collin, Miss Travel, and Miss Grace. The rest of the students were in their rooms. I had personally picked those students because they were worthy of trust. Miss Grace took the stand and said, "You have all been chosen for your loyalty and trustworthiness."

" Although secret forces and teams are forbidden, I trust that you will keep this meeting to yourself for your own safety. I have discovered some shocking evidence. I can't provide you with specific details, but I'll fill you in as much as I can," she explained.

"The authorities have created secret lethal weapons. They've created the lethal serum to terminate specific individual lives and the serum of destruction to terminate billions of lives. It could possibly terminate the whole human race. They intend to test the serum in Washington, D.C., a big city in the outside world, killing potentially 700,000 innocent people in two days," she added.

"They intend to eventually dominate the world by terminating the civil populations, depending on the results. Master Thunderstone gives the orders and doesn't care about deaths—or anybody for that matter. All he cares about is his power and throne," stressed Grace.

"Ashley and Mr. Corrigan are not the enemy; the authorities are. They made up a story for us to fear them, but it's a setup. Ashley and Mr. Corrigan are trying to fight the authorities. They have managed so far to destroy all their lethal weapons behind their backs, at great risk. But because they are now hunted, they are asking for your help to form a secret force and stop them. For those who are willing to fight, Mr. Corrigan invites you to fight with him. For those who'd rather not fight but want to participate in finding a way out of exile on this island, Ashley invites you to work with her. Those who are not interested in helping are free to go now."

They all looked at each other. Nobody moved. Nobody left. Finally Joshua said something.

"They killed my little brother for nothing. What kind of power and authority is that? It's personal for me. I want my revenge. Ashley saved my life more than once. She had plenty of opportunities to kill us if she wanted to. I trust Ashley more than Master Thunderstone. In fact, I owe her my life."

"She saved my life too," said Jackie.

"And mine," said Julius.

"She pretty much saved all of us. Without her, we would either be dead or still stuck in that terrible maze," added Mel.

"I hate to admit it. She may be powerful, but she is not dangerous. She was sent from the sky, that one. She is one-of-a-kind. I don't know what she is, but she is not evil," confessed Brad.

I was pretty touched by all of their recognition and praise. I felt some-what guilty all of a sudden. Guilty for not trying hard enough to make friends with anybody. I had put so many walls around myself, trying to protect myself from getting hurt again, that I forgot what friendship felt like. I suddenly missed my dear friend Antoinette. I knew that Veronica had desperately tried to make friends with me, and I didn't give her a chance...Mel and Julius too. I made a mental note to be more friendly with them; in fact, I owed them that much. They had been good to me, but I couldn't say the same thing from my side. I had been trying to avoid them most of the time. Now they were ready to fight the authorities with Collin and me. I was touched that they didn't want to turn me in.

"Where are Ashley and Mr. Corrigan?" asked Veronica.

"They are not ready to reveal their whereabouts until you have gained their trust. Needless to say, you are not to talk about this outside this group—not even to your best friend or your family. Ashley is asking you specifically, Veronica, not to say anything to Stephany. And Joshua, Mr. Corrigan would like to have Steven in our group, but Ashley thinks he is not worthy of trust. He puts you in charge determining whether he would be a good recruit without revealing anything to him. Use the death of your brother and the hunt for Ashley and Mr. Corrigan to initiate a talk with him. See what he thinks about it."

Joshua and Veronica nodded; they were sitting beside each other.

"Look at the people next to you. There are no barriers here, no matter what devotion house you're from. These are the people you can trust."

"What are we supposed to do?" asked Jackie.

"Go to sleep for now. I will call a meeting for tomorrow night at 9 p.m., same place. Meanwhile, watch your back and stay cool about all of this. The last thing you want to do is raise attention, so keep a low profile. We should have a plan by tomorrow night. Thank you for your help. Good night."

* * * * *

Steven and Joshua were talking on the hill at lunchtime. Joshua wasn't sure how to initiate the talk. I was sitting right beside them, but they didn't know. Collin was eavesdropping in the staff room for any kind of important information.

"Where do you think they are?" asked Joshua.

"Who?" replied Steven.

"Ashley and Mr. Corrigan."

"How should I know? My guess is in the forbidden forest."

"Do you think they are still alive?"

"Yes, otherwise the hunt would be over, right?"

"Do you really think they're dangerous?"

"I hate to give credit to a broad like that, but Ashley is very dangerous. Did you see all the shit she is able to do? I don't know what she is, but she isn't a witch. As for Mr. Corrigan, everybody seems shocked that he would be a traitor, but I'm not. People have a short memory. Just two years ago, he appeared on this island, acting weird and all. My dad doesn't like him either. He doesn't trust him. He never did."

"Who is your father?"

"Didn't you know? Seth Dawson."

"He is not the one who shot my brother?"

"Oh, shit, man. Don't look at it like that. It was a random shooting, nothing personal."

"It's kind of hard not to. They didn't have to shoot at anyone as far as I'm concerned."

"And that's why you will never be at the top of the work list, like my dad, with an attitude like that. Sometimes, you gotta do what you gotta do. Just friendly advice—stop questioning them, or they will hunt you down... just like Ashley and Mr. Corrigan."

* * * * *

Collin was in the hallway near the staff room, invisible. He waited a while before someone would walk out so he could peek inside. He was walking in the hallway when he saw Seth and Mr. Blake in the middle of a conversation. He went to eavesdrop.

"Of all the people, Collin doesn't surprise me at all. I knew he was trouble from the time he got to this island, but Miss Pomegrade? I didn't see that one coming," said Seth.

"Goes to show you that looks are deceiving," said Mr. Blake.

"Still no leads of their whereabouts?" asked Seth.

"No, nothing," Mr. Blake responded.

"Well, they can't be that far. They have nowhere to hide. We will find them," added Seth

"We'd better because we have other business to deal with. This is slowing us down with all this supervision. We have twenty-four hours to find them or our mission will be compromised," complained Mr. Blake.

Mr. Hunter came in and joined them.

"What are you talking about?"

"What do you think? About the hunted!" replied Mr. Blake.

"Oh, yes, what else. Too bad! She would have been a great witch. I have never seen a witch as bright and brave as her," said Mr. Hunter.

"Don't tell me you have a soft spot for her, now that she gave you the gold medal," said Seth.

"You know, at first I didn't like her, I didn't trust her. I felt threatened by her. But then I saw her in action. She truly is amazing. It was kind of refreshing and inspiring to see. She didn't look that dangerous to me. She saved many lives, after all."

"So why don't you find her and marry her? Make sure to invite us to the wedding..."

"All I said is that it's too bad to get rid of such talent, that's all. But whatever. You guys know what you are doing and what's best for this community."

"Damn right we do," said Seth.

* * * * *

I'd heard enough. There was no way we could include Steven in our army. I was sure Joshua felt it too. I still had half an hour before I would become visible again. Miss Grace had invited us to hide and wait in her bedroom. I decided not to waste my time hiding and went to the Grounding School to grab as many ingredients as possible and put them in my invisible backpack. We were getting low on invisibility serum and duplicate serum. I also wanted to secretly create the serum of ascendance, which would permit my soul to travel outside of my physical body. I had debated all this time if I should risk trying it, but now my heart was telling me it could be handy. My heart was also telling me not to mention or share this serum with anybody. When I went back to Miss Grace's room, I was relieved to see that nobody was there. I started to mix the ingredients to make the serums. I needed to crush the spirit crystal, but I didn't have a hammer. I knew there was one is the Grounding School. I made it fly my way. Once the crystal was crushed, I mixed in the rest of the ingredients. I remembered the instructions clearly. I knew I was taking a risk, that there was a chance I could die, but at least I would die trying. I wanted to go to the library and see if I could find an old formulas book where I could find the immune serum to escape the island. If not, I would have to go into the Master's office and spy. I drank the ascendant serum and lay in the bed. It didn't take long before I fell into a deep sleep.

I could see myself sleeping on the bed. My spirit was floating in the bedroom, so wasting no time, I flew to the library. The only one present was the old librarian. I wanted to ask him a question, but I knew I couldn't. I went from aisle to aisle. Finally, I found a 1914 formulas book on the second floor in the forbidden section. I looked around me. Nobody was there. I looked inside the book at the index. There it was: the immune serum. I read the page and took a mental picture of it.

The Immune Serum

This serum will enable you to cross any protection force field. You will be immune to any forbidden place for twenty-four hours. Not to be taken by children under twelve, pregnant woman, or people with heart disease or sensitive skin. May cause a rash, a migraine, and in rare cases a heart attack. To be taken with supervision.

Ingredients:

1 teaspoon of adrenaline abstract
1 tablespoon of morphine
1/2 cup of mud
1 cup of sea water
1 cup of fresh green algae
1/4 cup of tropical fish eggs

Mix all the ingredients into a paste. Eat one tablespoon. Makes 12 portions.

I put the volume back where it belonged and went explore in the Master's office. It was funny how my spirit knew where to go. The office was empty. I searched the surroundings. On his desk was a calendar. I looked for tomorrow's itinerary:

April 27

9 a.m.: arrival of the 50 trained dogs

10 a.m.: releasing dogs to sniff scents of Ashley and Collin in every single room

11 a.m.: meeting with Mr. Blake and his crew

12 p.m.: termination of Ashley and Collin with the lethal serum

3 p.m.: loading the helicopters

4:30 p.m.: lifting the seven layers of protective shields above the storage building

5 p.m.: launching of the helicopters

5:15 p.m.: replacing the protective shields

7 p.m.: diffusing Washington, D.C.

7:30 p.m.: returning to the island

9:15 p.m.: lifting the protective shields

9:30 p.m.: arrival on the island

9:45 p.m.: replacing the protective shields

I then searched for a safe. There was one behind a big picture of Master Thunderstone. There was no code number combination. Instead, it was protected with his eyeball scanner. The same for his entrance door.

I heard footsteps. I felt someone touching me and whispering into my ear, "Wake up, Ashley...Ashley?"

I knew it was time to go back into my body even though I didn't want to. I recognized Collin's panicked voice:

"Ashley? Are you OK? Come on, Ash, don't do this to me. Ashley?"

When I came back, I could feel the warmth of my body. I opened my eyes. My eyes met Collin's worried eyes. He was so close to my face. It gave me butterflies. He was so relieved when I looked at him. His face came closer to mine, and our lips joined together softly. I welcomed it. I remembered that I was supposed to be mad at him, but I had forgotten the reason why. I decided I didn't have time to be mad, time was running out. When he stopped kissing me, I said, "Hey! What's up?"

"God, you scared me. You were out. I couldn't wake you up. I thought you were dead."

"You worry too much. I'm fine. I was just sleeping."

"While you were having your beauty sleep, I found another recruit. You will never guess who it is."

I could. His mind was telling me, but I decided to play along.

"Who?"

"Mr. Hunter."

"What? Are you sure about this?"

"Yes. He likes you now. He could be a good asset for us."

"Yes, if we had the time....What time is it?"

"Around five last time I checked. I brought you a bag of food. I stole it from the cafeteria. I'm starting to like being invisible."

"Don't kid yourself. It won't last forever, but thanks, I'm starving."

We ate supper together. He told me about his day. I was quiet. I was only partly listening, I had too much on my mind.

"You are awfully quiet. Tell me about your day."

"Later. Miss Grace should be about to come, right?"

"Yes, why?"

"I want to try something."

"OK. I'm all yours," He looked at me with a funny look.

"Oh, don't be silly. It's not what you think. I want to see if I can put some kind of a protective shield in the room to prevent people from seeing or hear us."

"How could you do that?"

"I don't know. But I want to try. I guess we will find out when Miss Grace comes in."

I attempted the protective shield. A few minutes later, Miss Grace walked into her bedroom. She didn't acknowledge us. I waved in front of her and said, "Yoo-hoo, Miss Grace!"

No response.

Collin brought me right in front of Miss Grace and kissed me. She would for sure notice that and react. She didn't seem to see anything.

"So I heard you peed in your pants today, Miss Grace. What happened?" said Collin.

Still no response. Grace started to undress right in front of us, ready to take a shower. Collin laughed. I lifted the protection shield. When Grace saw us, she jumped and screamed. She covered herself with her opened blouse.

"What are you doing here? I was alone, and you guys just popped up in front of me."

Collin was laughing so much he had trouble speaking. "We were here the whole time. Genius here attempted a protective shield in your room, sight and sound, and she was testing to see if it worked."

"Well, you just about gave me a heart attack, but it worked."

"You really couldn't see or hear us?" I asked.

"No, not at all."

CHAPTER TWENTY-THREE

Once everybody was in for the 9 p.m. meeting, I put up a protective shield in the common room so that anybody else who came in or walked by wouldn't be able to see us or hear us. Then Collin and I came out of our hidden place. Their reactions were quite hilarious. They stood up, held their breath, and looked around to make sure nobody could see us.

"Hello, everyone. Don't worry, I put a protective shield around the room. Nobody can see or hear us. We are running out of time. Never mind recruiting more people, we have to act now. We can't afford to wait any longer," I said.

"We need to make a plan, together," said Collin.

"I discovered inside information that you should all know about. Tomorrow is still a go. They are going to attack Washington. I have seen the Master's schedule and made a copy for everybody."

I passed it on, and everybody looked at it.

"How did you come across it? Nobody has access to his office," Collin said.

"How I got it is not important. As you can see, we have to act now. I have good news though. I know where the secret access exit is on the island,

and I know how to make the immune serum to cross the seven layers of protective shields. The problem is how to get all the ingredients without getting caught. And we have to do it tonight. The sad part is that I will need one dose of the immune serum to go get the ingredients in the ocean," I said

"Only Master Thunderstone has access to it," said Collin.

"Exactly. It's in his office," I said to Collin.

"That is where you come in handy," I said to Miss Grace. "You will need to phone the Master and tell him you have seen us by the school. He will need to see it for himself. You will need to have some kind of evidence. You could take a picture of us on your phone, and you could show him our footsteps running toward the cafeteria. Once he is here, I will break into his office. I know where the safe is."

"How could you possibly break in? You will need his eyeball to break in!" said Miss Grace.

"Precisely. I will duplicate myself into Master Thunderstone."

Their reaction was priceless.

"Don't worry; I know how to do it. It will only take me five minutes at best to steal one flask. If I steal more than one, he will notice it, and God knows what he would do after. While I'm gone, I will need two volunteers to steal the entire adrenaline abstract from the Formula School as well as the morphine. Another person will need to get a full pail of mud. In the meantime, I will go into the ocean and pick up what I need."

"How can we go about this without being seen?" asked Joshua.

"By taking the invisible serum."

"That exists?" said Julius.

"Yes."

"I'm in. Anybody want to join me?" asked Joshua.

"I'll go," said Veronica before anybody else volunteered.

"I'll take the mud," said Mel.

"Ash, I can't let you do this by yourself. It's too risky," said Collin.

"I'll be fine. Meanwhile, the rest of you can come up with a plan on how to defy the authorities tomorrow, gather everybody on this island, and persuade them to escape and tell them how to deal with the dogs."

"I don't like this," said Collin.

"What other choice do we have?" I said. He didn't answer me. He knew I was right.

* * * * *

Once Master Thunderstone arrived on the front porch of the Teleportation School, I teleported in front of the Master's building. There were two security guards guarding the front entrance.

"Already back?" asked one of the guards.

"Yes. I forgot something. Wait until you get to be my age, you will see what I mean," I replied.

The scanner scanned my eye, and the front door opened. I had to again scan my eye in front of his office. It worked, and I walked in and went immediately to the safe. I again scanned my eye, and the safe unlocked. Just like I thought, there were rows of flasks. I read the label: Immune serum.

There was about one hundred flasks. I took one, drank it, and put the empty flask at the back. I closed the safe and walked out of his office. The door locked automatically. As soon as I was out of the building, I teleported to the ocean shore.

The waves calmed me down. It was very dark outside. I measured twenty cups of sea water into a big jar, and then I walked into the sea, looking for algae. It was hard to see. I finally stepped in something soft and slippery, and with some examination, I deduced that it was algae. I filled up two big Ziploc bags with algae.

I then looked for coral, hoping to find some tropical fish eggs. I held a flashlight in my hand. I was barefoot. After fifteen minutes of searching, I found coral and a school of bright tropical fish that swam away when they saw me. It was obvious where they had hidden their eggs. I grabbed as many eggs as I could and placed them in another jar. I then continued my search for more. I needed more if I wanted to save the whole island. After what seemed like forever, I put everything back into my backpack, which had become very heavy.

I knew I had been gone for a long time, so I drank some more invisible serum and made sure to pour a few drops on my backpack for extra precaution. I teleported into the Teleportation School's common room. It was empty and quiet. Too quiet. I had an uneasy feeling that something wasn't right, that something had gone wrong, but I had no time to waste. I needed the rest of the ingredients. I concentrated on the storage room in the Formula School and pictured where the adrenaline abstract and the morphine were. I made them fly into the common room. I was still invisible, so I decided to go take the mud myself.

"What's taking them so long? They should have been back by now," I said to myself. Mud in a pail, I teleported back into Miss Grace's room to work on the immune serum. After a good hour, I had created enough immune serum for two thousand portions; that was more than enough for this island. I looked at the time. It was midnight and still no sign of anybody. Where were they? Where was Collin? Now I knew something was wrong. I didn't know where to go or where to start looking. I chose to take the serum of ascension to go explore more easily.

I went in the Formula School to see if Joshua and Veronica were still there. The room was empty, but Veronica and Joshua had obviously been there. Their backpacks were on the floor in front of the storage shelving units. I didn't like this one bit. I decided to go to the jail. In one of the group cells were all my friends...all except Collin. They all looked worried and tired. Two guards were guarding the cell's entrance. In a corner was Veronica, crying on Joshua's shoulder. Miss Grace was pacing the room back and forth. Miss Travel was chewing her nails. Mel had a black eye. He obviously had been fighting. They didn't seem to be in immediate danger. I went to search for Collin. If the rest of them were here, shouldn't he be too? I went to the same room as the one where Miss Pomegrade had been killed. Sure enough, Collin was tied to a chair, beat up pretty badly. Seth and Mr. Blake were interrogating him, trying to discover where I was. Collin obviously wasn't saying anything; otherwise they would have killed him by now. They couldn't kill him until they knew where I was...at least I hoped so. I wanted to physically hurt them, but I couldn't. I was just a spirit. I had to go back into my body.

Back in my physical body, I stood up and drank the duplicate serum, picturing Master Thunderstone. I teleported in front of the jail. At the sight of me, the guards stood up straighter.

"Any updates on Ashley?" I asked them.

"Not that we know of," said one guard.

"May I come in?"

"Of course," said the other guard, opening the door for me.

As I walked in, I turned off the cameras with my mind. I went to the group cell.

"Master Thunderstone! What brings you here at this hour?" asked one of the guardians of the cell group.

Before the guards knew it, I attacked them unexpectedly. It was easy to knock them out. They both lay unconscious on the floor. I stole their keys and guns and opened the door for my friends.

"Ashley?" asked Miss Grace.

"Yes. Drink one teaspoon of that, all of you, and teleport to the shore. You should be safe; they won't look for you there," I said. "Once you drank the immune serum, you can teleport from here. Don't go outside the building this time." I gave Miss Grace two flasks. "It should be more than enough for all of them. Give them one teaspoon each," I said.

"Thanks. Where are you going?" asked Miss Grace.

"To save Collin. I'll meet you at the shore. Go, hurry before they find you!"

I walked to the death room. A single guard was guarding the door. He looked nervous seeing me.

"Open the door," I ordered.

"Yes, sir," the guard replied.

He opened the door. As soon as the door was halfway open, I knocked down the guard with one hard hit on the temple with the gun. He fell to the ground.

"Stop it!" I ordered to Seth and Mr. Blake.

"Sir?" asked Mr. Blake.

"I'll take it from here. Anybody watching from the mirror tonight?"

"No, sir. You said it wasn't necessary…"

"That's right. Now go take a break."

Once their backs were turned, I threw the two guns hard and with precision at both of their temples and knocked them down. I then tied them, as well as the guard from the hallway, to the chair with duct tape. Collin could barely open his eyes, they were so swollen. He couldn't talk either; his mouth was covered in blood. I untied him and said, "Drink this teaspoon and hold my hand. Hurry!" I held the spoon and put it in his mouth. He spilled most of the contents, so I gave him a second one. "Now be a good boy and drink all of this for me. I know you can do it. Hurry, before they wake up." He drank most of it this time. I took his hand and teleported to the shore. At the sight of us, our friends applauded. But when they saw how badly Collin was hurt, everybody went silent. I lay him down on the sand and started healing him. I didn't care who could see me this time. When Collin was completely healed, Miss Travel said, "What are you?"

"She's a lifesaver, my angel," responded Collin. And then he kissed me in front of everybody.

"Well, well, Collin! What about Antoinette?" teased Miss Grace.

"She was Antoinette," Collin said motioning to me.

"I should have guessed. She's just full of surprises. I guess you can now call me Grace outside of school," said Miss Grace. I smiled and nodded to her.

"What happened?" I asked them.

"As soon as we walked in the Formula School, the alarm went off, and we were locked in," said Veronica.

"Some kind of motion sensor, I think," said Joshua.

"Anyway, we couldn't teleport out or open the door. We were trapped," added Veronica.

"I was filling a pail of mud when I heard the alarm. I panicked. I went to tell Mr. Corrigan. We all teleported to the Grounding School for their rescue, but then we were all trapped when the guards came. They couldn't see us, but they had some kind of motion sensor. They knew we were there, and they waited, surrounding us like criminals. I punched one of the guards. He got me back pretty good. I backed off when I saw they had guns. Once the serum wore off, they handcuffed us and brought us to the cell," said Mel.

"Now what are we going to do?" asked Miss Travel.

"We have to fight back and try to escape with as many people as possible," said Collin.

"How can we do that? They will hunt us down now, all of us," said Karl.

"We can't leave without them. We need to blow up the island once everybody is gone," said Collin.

"But why?" asked Miss Travel.

"Because if we don't, they will continue to create the serum of destruction and destroy the world. This is not the world; it's only an isolated island. The world is much bigger," I said.

"Anybody got a plan?" Miss Grace said.

"How many people are on this island?" I asked.

"Last time I heard, it was 825 wizards," said Miss Grace.

"How many are not in this school zone?"

"About 250, I think."

"OK. We should start with the families with young kids. How about we split into three groups? One with the families, one with the students, and one with the village," I proposed.

"But if they see us, they will kill us," said Julius.

"Not if we all duplicate into Master Thunderstone. We would all carry a flask of immune serum and order them to drink one teaspoon and to teleport onto the shore. They will listen to the Master. Don't waste your time explaining anything. We have to do it now, tonight. We can't wait for tomorrow morning. You will all have one hour to convince your section before you become yourself again. You will have to closely watch the time and come back to the shore," I said.

"This is insane! I will not risk my life for this," said Miss Travel.

"Well, you can always stay behind and let the others do the work for you, like a queen would, if you want," said Collin impatiently. Miss Travel just looked at her feet, speechless.

"That means the rest of us, minus Miss Travel, will work on getting the students and Mr. Hunter. I'll take the Warriors dormitories. Mel, Julius, you take the Teleportation dormitories, and Ashley, the Formula dormitories. Miss Grace, go to the village, and Veronica and Joshua, the families. The rest of the authority people, they are all crooked. Let's not waste our time with them. They can die here," continued Collin.

I taught everyone how to take the duplicate serum. Shortly after, there were a dozen Master Thunderstones looking at each other. Julius said to the Master beside him, "Hey, man, you are one ugly old man with your long beard. Oh, and your breath skinks! I always wanted to tell you that!"

Everybody started laughing. It felt good. We needed that.

"Good luck, everyone! Don't forget to watch the time," I said before I teleported to the Formula devotion house.

CHAPTER TWENTY-FOUR

I teleported into every room, waking up the students. Most of them looked terrified. Nobody dared to question the Master, even though I could tell they didn't approve of it. They knew something didn't feel right. Once every student had teleported onto the shore, I went into Miss Bubbles's room and woke her up. She was insulted to be woken up in the middle of the night, saying, What is the meaning of this? What is so urgent that can't wait for tomorrow, sir?"

"Now is not the time. Don't question me. I'll explain everything soon. Now drink this and teleport onto the shore."

"But it's a forbidden place. We can't teleport there..."

"This with enable you to do so. Now hurry, Miss Bubbles. Stop wasting my time."

Once she was gone, I went into Mr. Hunter's room. He was snoring so loudly he sounded like a bear. It took me a while to wake him up. When he did, he was startled and jumped out of his bed, ready to attack me. But when he saw that it was Master Thunderstone, he dropped his arms.

"To what do I owe this honor in the middle of the night, sir?"

"I need you to drink this immune serum and teleport with me onto the shore."

"Can't it wait until the morning?"

"No. Hurry, I want to show you something. It's urgent."

"Very well then."

He drank the serum, and together we teleported to the shore. Every second, more and more people arrived. The shore was packed full of people. When a second and then a third Master Thunderstone teleported shortly after me, people started to panic.

"What the hell is going on here?" asked Mr. Hunter.

I asked a young student nearby if I could borrow his ring. He didn't want to lend it to me, but gave it anyway, out of fear. I put it near my mouth and used it as a microphone.

"May I have your attention please? Please, don't be alarmed. I know this is very unusual, but if you bear with me, I will explain everything. We are not the real Master Thunderstone. It's just a disguise to get your immediate attention. Pretty soon, our true identities will be revealed," I said.

I could feel the serum wearing off. A couple of seconds later, we became our true selves.

"Don't be alarmed. I am trying to save your lives. Master Thunderstone and the authorities have created a lethal serum as well as a serum of destruction. The purpose of these serums is to terminate innocent lives. The serum of destruction was created to terminate a whole human race. Tomorrow Master Thunderstone and his crew are going to hit the city of Washington D.C., killing about 700,000 innocent lives. If the mission is successful, he intends to terminate the human race, one continent at a time, and dominate the world."

Everybody looked stunned, and I continued with my speech. I didn't have any time to waste.

"I have created the immune serum to save everybody's lives. I have found the secret access to teleport us outside the island."

"Why would we want to teleport outside this island if they are going to destroy the world?" asked Mr. Hunter.

"Good question. We have created an antidote for those serums. The authorities are not aware of this. Tomorrow's mission will fail. Once they realize that the serum didn't work, they will think that their serum has been contaminated, and they will create more uncontaminated serum. They have the recipe. That's why you need to teleport out into the real world, where you will be safe. Once everybody has safely teleported out, we will destroy this island, to make sure this will never happen again, to make sure they will never destroy the world."

"Where will we go? We don't have anything with us," asked a mother with a baby in her arms.

"To the United States Immigration House. They will feed you, shelter you, and clothe you until you find a job. It's a good system. Now I can't force you to come with me, but if you stay, you will die. We will destroy the island, so you really don't have much of a choice. Now, in groups of twenty people, you will teleport onto the roof of the storage building… just say the name of the building. Once you are on the roof, you will teleport to the United States Immigration House. Every minute, I will send another group away. I will meet you on the other side. Now team up in groups of twenty. The first group will teleport with Miss Grace. She will guide you from there."

Miss Grace nodded to me. One group at a time teleported to the storage roof, then to the Immigration House. Every minute, I sent another group. We could hear dogs barking from afar, searching for me. Forty-five minutes later, I sent the last group. Just Collin and I were left, as planned. We intended to teleport a missile onto the roof of the storage building just as we teleported out. The island would then be destroyed. There were thirty seconds left. He took my hand and kissed me gently. Then, all of a sudden, something black hit us hard and teleported us back onto the island. We were tied to a chair with duct tape in a dark room. We couldn't teleport out. The first thing we saw was Master Thunderstone.

"Gotcha!" he said.

His mind was telling me that instead of teleporting outside the island, Steven had teleported to his dad's room and told him our plan.

"Now you will finally die."

He threw a diffuser in the room. It caught me by surprise; I didn't see this one coming. We were instantly put in a deep coma.

My soul was flying in the sky, toward a bright light. Collin's soul was right beside me. We were heading the same way. He looked at me. He smiled and winked at me. I winked back. Once we were back at our soul school, our soul group friends gave us high fives.

"Well, it took you long enough to figure this out!" Victor teased me again. I recognized him. He was the joker of the group.

"Last time, you two were enemies. Now you are lovers. Go figure," he added.

"Nice to see you, Ashley," said a soft voice.

I turned my head toward the voice. I couldn't help but smile when I saw her.

"Antoinette!"

I ran into her arms.

"You've done well, Ashley. You've saved many lives."

"But I didn't save you."

"Are we back to this? I thought we had turned the page on this," she said.

I wanted to continue to chat with my best friend, but I felt myself being pulled away. I was slowly waking up. A deep voice was heard in the sky.

"My dear child! Come see me! Just follow the bright light."

I recognized this voice. It was my father. Although it saddened me to leave Antoinette, I was happy to see him just the same. As I approached the bright light, I also became light. It was electrifying. My father, the Sun, was greeting me with his warmth and his pure energy. I suddenly remembered who I was. I was a child of the sun. I was the youngest of the twelve children.

"At last! My child, I am so proud of you. You did well. You were not poisoned by your powers like your brothers and sisters. You are the only successful one so far in this lifetime. Now I need you to go back to earth, finish your mission, and then I will have a second mission for you: Bring your brothers and sisters back to me."

"Father, I am always at your service. But could you let me rest a little before you give me the details of my second mission? I have a feeling it's going to be complicated."

"Ha! Ha! Ha! Indeed it will be. Now go back in your body. Remember who you are and that I am always with you, wherever you go."

"Will I remember this time when I go back?"

"Do you really want to remember? It's a lot to take for a human."

"Yes, I really want to. Ashley is tough. She can take it."

"As you wish. I have faith in you."

"Can I bring Collin back with me?"

"Ah! Collin! I was afraid you would say that. He is not our kind, but he is worthy of my trust. He is a star seed, a being who already achieved higher consciousness on other planets. That is why he is in the same soul group as you. He was sent to the planet earth, a place of service, with his own mission. He can help you."

I bowed to him and blew him a kiss, and then I went back to my soul's school and grabbed Collin's hand and started walking away from our soul group.

"We are not done, are we?" asked Collin.

"Not quite."

Together we flew back into our bodies.

CHAPTER TWENTY-FIVE

We gasped for a deep breath when we came back into our bodies. Our bodies were aching, still unable to open our eyes. Our hearts started to beat regularly, our breathing too. After a while, our brain was activated again. When we came out of the coma, we were laying side by side, bolted in some kind of a cage, alone in the dark. We were slowly sinking in water. Pretty soon, our backs were completely immersed in the water. I felt weak and my head was killing me, but I still focused on the bolt and made it detach from the cage. I did the same to Collin, then I made the top of the cages open. We sat down, trying to catch our breath. I was exhausted and felt like I'd been hit by a train, but now was not the time to rest. I checked if I still had some immune serum securely taped on my belly. I did. I shared one flask with Collin. We teleported to the roof of the storage building. I asked my mind to fly a missile our way. Within five seconds, I saw something in the sky coming fast at us. Hand in hand, we teleported into the United States Immigration House. When we arrived, everybody stood up and applauded. The Immigration House was full. The staff was overwhelmed with all the unexpected strangers. They didn't have enough supplies for everyone.

"Why don't you ask the Red Cross to come and help you?" I suggested.

"Good idea," said a worker.

"What took you so long? We thought we lost you or that you had abandoned us," Miss Grace said.

"Things got complicated, but we made it," replied Collin.

While Collin was explaining the events, I had something else on my mind. I walked toward a staff lady.

"May I use your washroom?" I asked.

"Go ahead. Second door on the left."

I went into an empty stall and sat comfortably on the toilet. I took a dose of ascendance serum. I closed my eyes.

I flew above the ocean, toward the island. I needed to make sure my mission was completed. The island was nowhere to be found. It had been destroyed. Some residue was floating in the ocean. I flew closer. Pieces of trees and wood were floating. No survivors in sight. Good. Mission accomplished. I flew back into my body.

I splashed some water on my face before I went back to the crowd.

"Are you OK?" asked Collin, taking my two hands. Collin looked as exhausted as I did. We both needed to rest.

"Yes. I'm going home. Want to join me?"

"No. I'd rather stay here with a way too full house…just kidding," he teased me.

We said good-bye and good luck to the people and hugged our new friends. We promised to come back and see them soon before we teleported to my old house's porch. I knocked nervously to the door.

"Try to act normal OK?" I said to Collin.

He looked at me with a funny smile.

"Relax; I was born in this country too. I know the drill."

The door opened. We couldn't believe our eyes when we saw Master Thunderstone at the door. I could see my parents tied up in the background with duct tape on their mouth. They both looked frightened, and my mom was crying.

"Gotcha!" said Master Thunderstone.

ABOUT THE AUTHOR

Mélanie C. Larue is an elementary teacher. She published her first novel For a Brief Moment in 2013, a fiction book for adults, then a second fiction novel Hidden in the Bush in 2014. In November 2015, she published her first fantasy novel for YA, Child of the Sun, the first of a series of two. Her second novel of the series, Children of the Sun, will soon be released.